Dear Reader,

We're constantly striving to bring you the best romance fiction by the most exciting authors...and in Harlequin Romance® we're especially keen to feature fresh, sparkling, warmly emotional novels. Modern love stories to suit your every mood—poignant, deeply moving stories; lively upbeat romances with sparks flying; or sophisticated, edgy novels with an international flavor.

All our authors are special, and we hope you continue to enjoy each month's new selection of Harlequin Romance novels. We're proud to feature international bestselling Harlequin Presents author **Carole Mortimer**, who makes a special guest appearance in Harlequin Romance this month! Carole has more than 50 million books in print worldwide—her strong characters and dramatic stories keep readers enthralled until the very last page. In *The Fiancé Fix*, Carole has created a tantalizing feel-good story with a gripping emotional dilemma....

We hope you enjoy this book by **Carole Mortimer**—and look out for future sparkling stories in Harlequin Romance. If you'd like to share your thoughts and comments with us, do please write to:

Harlequin Romance
Eton House,18-24 Paradise Road
Richmond, Surrey
TW9 1SR, U.K.

or e-mail us at: Tango@hmb.co.uk.

Happy reading!
The Editors

Carole Mortimer says, "I was born in England, the youngest of three children—I have two older brothers. I started writing in 1978, and have now written over ninety books for Harlequin.

"I have four sons—Matthew, Joshua, Timothy and Peter— and a bearded collie called Merlyn. I'm in a very happy relationship with Peter senior. We're best friends as well as lovers, which is probably the best recipe for a successful relationship. We live on the Isle of Man."

CAROLE MORTIMER
The Fiancé Fix

TANGO

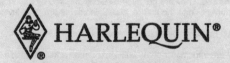

HARLEQUIN®

TORONTO • NEW YORK • LONDON
AMSTERDAM • PARIS • SYDNEY • HAMBURG
STOCKHOLM • ATHENS • TOKYO • MILAN • MADRID
PRAGUE • WARSAW • BUDAPEST • AUCKLAND

My Husband,
Peter

ISBN 0-373-03719-8

THE FIANCÉ FIX

First North American Publication 2002.

Visit us at www.eHarlequin.com

Printed in U.S.A.

CHAPTER ONE

'Is THIS place only for women, or do you do men as well?'

Now, there was a leading question, Joey thought humorously, looking up from the money she had been counting in the till at the end of a long working day.

Wow! The man standing in the doorway might not have a way with words, but his looks more than made up for it: tall and muscular, with a ruggedly handsome face, shaggy dark hair, and come-to-bed eyes the same colour as melted brown chocolate.

Joey paused; now, where had that last thought come from? She was a thirty-year-old single mother with a six-year-old daughter. During the last ten years or so she thought she had heard every chat-up line in the book—she had certainly never been attracted to a man because of the unspoken message in his eyes—the opposite in fact!

She straightened. 'This is a unisex hair salon, if that's what you're asking,' she answered drily.

His mouth twisted. 'That's what I was asking,' he confirmed wryly. 'Do you have the time to do something with his?' He ran a rueful hand through the thickness of his dark, unruly hair.

In fact, the salon had closed at five-thirty, five minutes ago, but Susie, the last assistant to leave, must have forgotten to put the catch down on the door on her way out.

'Actually, we're closed—'

'I'm sorry to have bothered you.' The man nodded, turning to leave.

'—but if you're only wanting a trim...?' Joey finished

with a questioning rise of her blonde brows. It was Lily's evening for ballet, so Joey didn't actually have to leave to collect her for another half an hour or so.

'That's great!' The man did such a quick about-face as he strode back into the salon, closing the door behind him as he did so, that Joey took a step backwards.

He certainly wasn't backward in coming forward! And in the confines of the modern salon, with its black and chrome decor, posters of the latest hairstyles adorning the walls, the man's sheer size was even more noticeable. Broad shoulders in a checked work shirt, tapered waist, long legs in blue, slightly dusty denims—the man had to be well over six feet tall.

Maybe this wasn't such a good idea after all, Joey worried as she came out from behind the reception desk; despite his size, the man seemed friendly enough, but the two of them were very much alone in here, and even serial killers could probably be charming!

'Believe me, I'm only interested in having my hair trimmed,' the man reassured her as he settled himself down in one of the chairs that faced the mirrored wall.

Joey's face flamed with embarrassment. So much for the cool sophisticate she believed herself to be; one look at her expression, and this man had known exactly what she was thinking!

She took down one of the protective wraps hanging on the rail behind her and draped it around him, effectively trapping his hands beneath its folds; a rose-pink wrap usually set aside for female clients. Two could play at this game!

'Now, what would you like done?' she enquired in her most professional voice, looking at his reflection in the mirror, dismissing the realisation of how tiny she looked standing next to him. Only as tall standing as he was sitting down, her shoulder-length blonde hair cut in a shaggy easy-to-manage style, guarded green eyes surrounded by dark lashes as they met his gaze levelly.

He shrugged. 'As I said, just a trim.'

He had very nice hair, as chocolate-brown as those teasing eyes. If a little dusty, she discovered as she ran her hands professionally through the healthy brown waves.

'Would you like your hair washed before I cut it?' she offered lightly.

'I'll wash it later when I shower,' he refused with a grimace. 'If you don't mind the fact I'm a little dusty, that is?' He raised dark brows.

'Not at all.' Joey turned away to pick up her comb and scissors, having noticed on closer proximity that he gave off an odour of aftershave, with an underlying masculine smell of sweat usually engendered by physical labour. 'Are you working on the building site next door?' she asked conversationally as she began to cut his hair.

He nodded. 'I really am sorry I'm such a mess,' he grimaced again. 'Ordinarily, I would never have come in here straight from work, but—'

'You have a heavy date tonight?' Joey guessed teasingly—looking like this, when wouldn't this man have a 'heavy date'?

'Something like that.' He chuckled softly, a deep, throaty sound that made Joey's nerve-endings tingle.

Much to her disquiet. Really, this man had just walked in here off the street, was obviously a building labourer, probably a transient worker; the chances were Joey would never see him again after today. Besides, he had a 'heavy date' this evening...

'How are things progressing over there?' She nodded in the direction of the building site behind the salon.

'Not bad. This place will be coming down soon too, won't it?' he queried lightly.

Joey's fingers faltered slightly as she shaped the hair over his ears, glad she was bending forward so that he couldn't see her expression clearly. 'Soon, yes,' she confirmed hardly.

She tried not to think about it, despite the fact that her landlord had informed her several weeks ago that he wouldn't be renewing her lease when it came to an end in two months' time.

Like everyone else in this block of buildings, he had sold out to the Mason supermarket chain. A supermarket chain rapidly becoming the biggest in the country, and so able to pay her landlord a much larger sum than he would ever receive in rent, even over a hundred-year period! In fact all of the other properties in this particular square were already empty, or in some cases demolished.

This man might be slightly dusty, but the salon had been in a similar condition since the first building came down several weeks ago, dust covering every surface no matter how often it was cleaned.

'Sore point?' the man in front of her prompted softly.

'Yes.' Joey didn't even attempt to prevaricate; 'sore' didn't begin to describe how she felt over effectively being evicted. 'I realise you work for Dominic Mason,' she sighed, 'but—'

'The building work for the new supermarket is contracted out to Harding Construction,' he cut in.

'Whatever,' Joey dismissed—what did it matter who built the damned thing? The fact that she was having to find new premises for her business was still causing a major upheaval in her life.

As if she needed another one just now! Lily's father had crawled out of the woodwork two months ago too. In fact, she had received notification that her lease wouldn't be re-newed and the letter from Lily's father on the very same day. A black day in her life!

The first, in view of the fact that her lease was coming to an end anyway, it appeared she could do nothing about. The second she had dealt with by way of a very abrupt letter informing Daniel Banning that she had absolutely nothing to say to him, that anything that needed to be said had already been done so. The silence since she had sent that letter had been oppressive.

'You were saying…?' her customer prompted curiously. 'About Dominic Mason,' he reminded her as Joey looked at his reflection blankly.

Dominic Mason, Joey thought disgustedly. Since his appearance in the supermarket line ten years ago the man had managed to buy out two other prominent chains, expanding to the States and Europe, as well as increasing his own chain in England.

'The man will only be happy when he owns every supermarket in the world,' she gritted.

'A supermarket megalomaniac,' the man said with knowing humour.

'Exactly,' Joey agreed, easily getting into full stride where the subject of Dominic Mason was concerned. 'Just how much money does one man need?' she scorned, snipping away at the dark hair. 'He—'

'Not too short, if you don't mind,' the man put in softly.

'Sorry.' She gave him a rueful smile, easing up on the cutting. 'As you've probably guessed, Dominic Mason is not my favourite person.'

'Hardly surprising, really.' The man nodded. 'Has your boss found somewhere else to go yet?'

Boss…?

'*I'm* the "Joanne" over the shop front,' she corrected

him. 'Although everyone calls me Joey,' she added—for some reason she wasn't completely sure of. Her friends called her Joey—and this man was far from being that!

'I hadn't realised you're actually the owner,' he admitted. 'No wonder you're p—er—not feeling very happy—' he amended whatever he had been about to say '—with Dominic Mason.'

'He'll win in the end, of course,' she sighed, brushing away the cut hair from the back of his neck. 'His sort always do. But I don't intend moving from here until I absolutely have to,' she added resolutely.

She knew that her salon was probably causing problems to the building of the new Mason supermarket, standing as it did almost in the middle of the construction site! Good—any nuisance value she could give Dominic Mason was worth all the dust she had to contend with every day!

'I can't say that I blame you,' the man acknowledged lightly, standing up once Joey had removed the pink wrap. 'How much do I owe you?'

'It's eight pounds fifty for a trim,' she related automatically, glancing at the serviceable watch on her wrist; nearly time to pick up Lily and her friend Daisy from ballet; it seemed flowers had been the fashion in girls' names six years ago!

'Damn!' He had reached into his jeans pocket, the hand coming out empty. 'I remember now. I left my wallet in my other clothes.' He groaned. 'A building site isn't exactly the ideal place to carry money and credit cards.'

Great. Now it turned out the man couldn't even pay her for the haircut! As for his 'other clothes', the dusty jeans and shirt looked as if he had been wearing them for some time. Not that this was the first time something like this had happened to her, but it was usually one of Joey's regular customers who had simply left their purse at home by mistake.

'Look, I'm really sorry about this,' the man apologised, dark colour staining the hardness of his cheeks. 'Is it OK if I drop the money in first thing in the morning?'

'Fine,' Joey answered, sure she wasn't going to see this man—or the money—the next day.

Not that she was a cynic, exactly; it was just that life had a habit of throwing unexpected curves at her. Being taken in by this man was just one more thing to add to an already lengthy list!

'You don't believe me, do you?' he realised slowly as he studied her with narrowed eyes.

Joey gave him a quick smile. 'I said it's fine.' After all, it had been her own time she had been wasting! Time, she realised after a second glance at her watch, that she no longer had to waste.

'I hope I haven't kept you from anything?' He had obviously seen that second glance at her wristwatch.

'Not at all,' she assured him lightly. 'And please don't give paying for the haircut another thought.' She waved a dismissive hand.

'I've said I'll pay you in the morning, and I will,' he assured her grimly. 'I should lock this door after me, if I were you,' he advised firmly.

Come-to-bed eyes *and* a caring nature...! Quite an attractive combination.

No way, Joey, she immediately reproved herself. There were enough complications in her life already—finding new premises for her salon, as well as fending off Daniel Banning's attempts to disrupt the life she had painstakingly built for Lily and herself—without finding herself attracted to a man who had a 'heavy date' this evening—and who didn't even have the money to pay for his haircut!

'Thanks.' She followed him over to the door.

He turned in the doorway. 'I really will be by first thing in the morning to pay you,' he repeated.

'Of course you will.' She nodded, unconvinced.

His mouth tightened at her obvious scepticism. 'What time do you open?'

'Nine-thirty. But, as I've already said, don't worry about it—'

'Oh, but I will,' he cut in softly. 'It will probably keep me awake all night,' he teased, before striding off to get into the dusty pick-up parked outside.

Joey gave a derisive snort as she watched him drive away; he might not get any sleep tonight, but she had a definite feeling it would have more to do with his 'heavy date' than it would worrying over the fact that he owed her eight pounds fifty!

'OK, Daisy, we're home,' Joey told her young charge drily. The two young girls seated in the back of the car were talking so much that she was sure neither of them was aware they had reached Daisy's home.

Joey wouldn't mind, but the two girls saw each other every day at school, and for a couple of hours afterwards, but as soon as tea and homework were over Lily would be on the telephone to her best friend, talking away as if the two girls hadn't seen each other for weeks!

Had she ever been like that? Joey wondered ruefully. She didn't think so. But, for all her faults, her mother had at least been waiting at home for her every day when she came home. Both being children of single mothers, neither Lily or Daisy had that...

'Thanks.' Daisy grinned at her before scrambling out of the back of the car.

'Tell your mother I'll be here to pick you up at eight-thirty in the morning,' Joey told her automatically, returning Hilary's wave as the other woman came out of the house to greet Daisy.

Both on their own, the two women shared the responsibility of their two daughters while they juggled the careers they needed to support them—Joey driving the girls to school in the morning, Hilary picking them up in the afternoons and keeping Lily with her until Joey picked her up after work. The arrangement had worked very well so far.

'Did you have a good day, Mummy?' Lily asked interestedly as they drove the extra mile to their own home. She was a tiny replica of Joey—thank goodness Joey could see none of her father in her!

Joey frowned. Until five-thirty it had been like all the other days she had had recently—busy, and dusty. Until she had been taken in by that— But there was no reason to bother Lily with that.

'It was fine, darling,' she responded lightly. 'How about you?'

Her daughter's face was screwed up when Joey glanced at her in the driving mirror. 'I've brought my spelling test home for Friday.'

Joey held back a smile; the trouble with schoolwork was that it got in the way of Lily's social life!

'I'm sure we'll cope,' she promised, straight-faced. 'Now, what do you fancy for tea today?'

'Pasta and chicken nuggets,' her daughter answered predictably—she very rarely willingly ate anything else.

Joey smiled indulgently. 'I think we'll put a few peas with that, don't you?' she teased—Lily's aversion to vegetables was universal in children her age.

'If you have to,' her daughter allowed grudgingly. 'I—

Oh, look, Mummy, there's a car parked outside our house,'
she said excitedly.

Joey frowned as she looked at the blue car parked at the
roadside; visitors were few and far between to the tiny end-
terrace house the two shared in a quiet residential part of
town. Between work and caring for Lily, with all that en-
tailed, there was very little time for a social life of her own.

'Perhaps they're visiting next door,' she dismissed, parking her own car behind the blue one before getting out and
opening the back door for Lily, deliberately not paying too
much attention to the parked car. Just because they rarely
received visitors that was no reason to stare at the car as if
it were a vehicle from outer space!

Her daughter felt no such inhibitions, openly ogling the
car as she held on to Joey's hand and they walked to their
front door. 'There's a man sitting inside, Mummy,' she told
Joey in a stage whisper.

Joey winced at the loudness of her daughter's voice, sure
the 'man sitting inside' the car must have heard her. After
all, the car engine was switched off, and it was a warm
evening, so the man probably had the window down too.

She unlocked their front door before pushing it open.
'Come on, Lily' she encouraged as her daughter still hung
back curiously.

'He's getting out of the car, Mummy,' Lily informed her
even as she pulled on the sleeve of the light jacket Joey
wore over a pink T-shirt and black trousers.

Joey could see that for herself, her gaze narrowing
against the evening sunshine as she watched the man slowly
unfolding his long length from inside the car.

Tall and blond, with a smoothly handsome face dominated by a pair of analytical blue eyes that raked over her
in cool assessment, before moving down to stare openly at

Lily. Joey felt as if she had had all the breath kicked out of her as she instantly recognised him.

Lily's father.

The ominous feeling that had dogged her for the weeks following her terse letter in reply to his own came back in full force.

Because Joey knew, as she put a protective arm about Lily and pulled her daughter close against her, there could be only one reason why Daniel had come here...

CHAPTER TWO

'GO INSIDE and hang up your school blazer, Lily,' Joey told her daughter shakily. 'I'll join you in a few minutes.'

'But, Mummy—'

'Go inside, Lily!' she snapped, before drawing in a deep controlling breath, forcing herself to smile reassuringly as her daughter's bottom lip wobbled precariously at her unexpected terseness. 'I'll be in shortly,' she assured her lightly. 'Go and put a video on for a while,' she encouraged, knowing this unexpected treat after school would soothe Lily's ruffled feelings; usually television and videos were banned until the weekend.

'Great!' Lily enthused, before rushing into the house without a backward glance, their unexpected visitor already forgotten.

At least, by Lily...

Joey tensed once her daughter was safely inside the house, her shoulders straightening as she raised her head to look across at the man who had created this scene.

She narrowed her gaze, her expression one of puzzlement as she looked at him fully. 'You aren't Daniel,' she realised slowly.

Oh, this man was very like Lily's father—both men tall and blond, both having those cool, calculating blue eyes—but this man was older than the thirty-two Daniel would now be, was probably aged in his late thirties or early forties. But the likeness between the two men was enough for Joey not to feel entirely reassured by this fact...

16

'My name is *David* Banning.' The man spoke with a hard American drawl. 'I'm Daniel's brother.'

Daniel's brother... Joey hadn't even known he had a brother. Although she had no reason to doubt this man's word. Besides, the likeness was unmistakable.

'Daniel didn't have the nerve to show his face here himself, then?' she scorned.

The blue gaze became even more icy, the hard mouth tightening into a thin line. 'That would have been rather difficult, in the circumstances,' David Banning rasped harshly. 'Daniel died four months ago!'

Joey could only stare uncomprehendingly at David Banning after he made this blunt announcement, unable to take in what he had just said, swallowing hard, swaying slightly, knowing a sudden feeling of light-headedness.

Daniel was dead...?

But how—? What...?

She shook her head as a sudden thought occurred to her. 'He can't be,' she denied weakly. 'I... He wrote to me. Just two months ago—'

'That was me,' David Banning interrupted.

D. Banning. The letter she had received had been signed 'D. Banning'. This man, Daniel's brother, was D. Banning too...

She had thought the signature on the letter a little formal, given the circumstances, but, as Daniel hadn't been seen since the moment he was informed of Lily's birth, Joey had decided he really was the stranger he obviously preferred to be.

But the letter hadn't been from Daniel at all. Because he had already been dead two months when the letter was sent...

'How did he die?' she breathed huskily.

His brother shrugged dismissively. 'The same way he

lived—recklessly,' he said harshly. 'He was driving a high-speed motorboat—too fast—when it flipped over and sank. We recovered his body three days later,' he added.

Joey thought back to the fun-loving, irresponsible man she had known seven years ago. Yes, she could see Daniel enjoying the power of going along on the water at high speed, could almost hear that huskily triumphant laugh of his as he challenged the sea gods.

And lost...

'I'm sorry,' she murmured dazedly.

'Are you?' his brother questioned sceptically. 'I think the two of us need to talk, don't you?' he added hardly.

Joey stiffened defensively. She didn't like the sound of that at all. This man had already told her all that she needed to know—hadn't he...?

'As you can see, I'm rather busy at the moment.' She nodded vaguely in the direction of the house, the sound of the video playing inside audible in the quiet of early evening.

'As I can see,' David Banning echoed softly, moving around the car to stand only feet away from her, his light suit obviously expensively tailored, as was the white silk shirt and grey tie he wore beneath it. 'She's very like Daniel,' he murmured huskily.

Joey recoiled at the claim. '*She* is called Lily,' she snapped coldly. 'And she is absolutely nothing like Daniel. Thank God!'

'Just so,' David Banning acknowledged with a mocking inclination of his head. 'But I still say we need to talk—Josey, isn't it?' he drawled knowingly.

'Joey,' she corrected abruptly, desperately trying to take all of this in.

Just how much did this man know of what had happened

seven years ago? And exactly what did he want to do about it?

'Joey,' he repeated with a hard smile. 'I realise all this has probably been—a shock for you,' he drawled. 'I also accept that you're tied up with…Lily at the moment, and that our conversation would be better taking place where she can't be a witness to it.' He frowned thoughtfully. 'Perhaps you could meet me later this evening and we could go somewhere quiet and have dinner together—'

'No!' she cut in harshly. 'No,' she repeated more calmly as he looked at her with raised brows. 'It isn't possible to organise a babysitter at such short notice. Besides—'

'Besides, you don't want to have dinner with me later,' David Banning finished. 'I've come over from the States for the sole purpose of talking to you, Joey—'

'My name is Delaney,' she cut in forcefully. 'Miss Delaney,' she added pointedly. 'I don't know you well enough for you to call me Joey.'

She hadn't known the man at the salon earlier well enough, either, came the unbidden thought, and yet she had invited him to use the familiarity! In retrospect, the fact that he owed her eight pounds fifty for a haircut was nothing when put into perspective with the damage this other man could wreak in her life!

'Miss Delaney,' David Banning mused mockingly. 'It's Irish, isn't it?'

'So what if it is?' she challenged defensively.

'No reason.' He shrugged. 'Let's make it tomorrow evening, then,' he continued hardly, his tone brooking no argument to what wasn't even meant to sound like a suggestion.

Joey was aware that she had been outside talking to him on the pavement for over ten minutes already, and Lily wouldn't remain enthralled in her video for long if Joey failed to appear. But she didn't want to meet this man to-morrow evening!

'I'm staying at the Grosvenor Hotel.' He named the best hotel in town—although it was obvious from his tone that it didn't come up to his usual standards.

Joey knew from Daniel that the Bannings were a very prominent banking family in New York, and that they lived up to that lifestyle one hundred per cent; obviously the little town in which Joey had chosen to make her home, with its three-star hotel, didn't quite meet those standards!

'That's nice for you,' she returned sarcastically.

David Banning's mouth tightened at her obvious scorn. 'I was suggesting that we meet there tomorrow evening for dinner,' he rasped.

He hadn't been 'suggesting' anything—it had been in the nature of an order! But the Grosvenor wasn't a place Joey knew well, and the chances were that no one there would know her, either... Besides, she doubted this man would go away until he had spoken to her.

'Very well,' she accepted abruptly. 'I'll meet you there at eight o'clock tomorrow evening.' She was sure the neighbour's teenage daughter, who usually babysat for her on the rare occasions she went out, would be only too pleased to earn some extra money. 'Now, if that's all...?' she added pointedly.

'For the moment.' He gave an abrupt inclination of his head.

'Who was that man, Mummy?' Lily turned to ask curiously when Joey entered the sitting-room a few minutes later.

'Just a salesman trying to sell me something,' Joey dismissed tersely; Lily had never known her father—she certainly didn't need to know that the man outside was his brother! 'Tea will be ready in fifteen minutes,' she added lightly, before escaping to the kitchen.

Once there she took some time to gather her scattered thoughts together. The D. Banning who had written to her had been Daniel's brother David, not Daniel himself. And now he had travelled all the way from America for the sole purpose of talking to her. There could be only one subject he wanted to discuss with her—Lily!

Well. Joey straightened decisively. He could say whatever it was he wanted to say, and then leave. Neither she nor Lily needed anything from him.

'There's a man in the salon asking to see you, Joey,' Hilary told her lightly as she came out back into the tiny room Joey occasionally used as an office.

Joey instantly paled. David Banning! He hadn't waited for dinner this evening, after all. Why hadn't he? What had happened that he needed to see her so early this morning? It would be too much to hope that he had come to inform her he had to return urgently to the States!

'Thanks, Hilary.' She gave her assistant and friend a shaky smile as she reluctantly stood up.

The two women had met a year ago, when Hilary came to the salon for a job, and within weeks of working together the two women had worked out their system—Hilary finished work at the salon at three-fifteen every weekday, so that she could go to the school to collect Lily and Daisy, and cared for Lily at her home until Joey finished at the salon for the day. It was a system that worked well for both women.

'He's rather gorgeous,' Hilary murmured admiringly.

Joey had barely noticed David Banning's good looks the evening before, but, yes, she supposed he was rather handsome. If you liked cold self-confidence that bordered on arrogance, that was. Joey didn't—had been completely cured of that romantic image seven years ago when Daniel, also arrogantly confident, had walked out on them!

'Perhaps,' she answered noncommittally, moving around her desk to follow Hilary out into the salon, bracing herself for this second meeting with Daniel's brother.

Her eyes widened with surprise as she saw the man waiting there. Not David Banning, after all, but the man from the previous evening who hadn't been able to pay for his haircut!

He looked slightly less disreputable today, the shirt and denims looking relatively clean, at least.

'You weren't expecting me,' he said slowly as he took in Joey's surprised expression.

No, she hadn't been, had been sure she'd been taken for a ride the evening before. But she was relieved to see that it was him rather than the man she *had* been expecting!

'I told you I would be in this morning to pay for my haircut,' he reminded her mockingly, handing her a ten-pound note.

Joey gave a shaky smile. 'That's very kind of you.' She nodded, taking the money and putting it in the till.

The unexpected honesty had also gone some way to restoring her faith in human nature. Now, if she could just make David Banning go back to America without making any waves in her own or Lily's lives...!

'Keep the change,' the man told her dismissively as she would have given him one pound fifty back. 'We'll call it interest paid, if you like,' he added wryly.

'The last I heard interest wasn't as high as almost twenty per cent.' Joey smiled wanly.

The man returned the smile. 'Bad debts come slightly higher than normal— Hey, are you OK?' He looked at her closely. 'You look ill,' he added, his brown eyes narrowing consideringly on the paleness of her face.

Joey was instantly on the defensive. She had spent a terrible evening after putting Lily to bed, worrying about David Banning's visit here, and an even worse night as sleep evaded her, going over and over in her mind what Daniel's brother could possibly want from her. Ultimately she had arrived at answers that were completely unacceptable to her.

She knew she looked awful, despite the make-up she had applied earlier in an effort to hide her sleepless night. But she couldn't exactly say she appreciated this man commenting on the fact!

'Of course I'm OK,' she snapped irritably.

'You don't look it,' the man persisted, making no effort to leave, despite the fact that he had now paid his 'bad debt'.

Joey was aware of the fact that they were receiving curious looks. With the salon very busy at this time of the morning, staff and clients alike seemed more than a little interested in the conversation taking place between Joey and this ruggedly handsome man. And Hilary kept shooting them interested looks, even as she permed an elderly lady's hair.

'I really am fine, Mr—er—I'm fine,' she repeated firmly as she realised she didn't even know the man's name.

'Nick,' he told her tersely. 'And you aren't fine,' he refuted gently, taking a hold of her arm and turning her back in the direction of the tiny office she had just come from.

'Really, Mr—Nick,' she began indignantly. 'You can't just come in here and—'

'And what?' he prompted, releasing her once they were in the privacy of her office, the door firmly closed behind them. 'Show a little concern for someone who, obviously tired from a day's work last night, looks as if she had been run over by a steamroller?'

'Thanks!' Joey muttered drily, moving to sit behind the desk. She would feel better with a little distance between the two of them; her arm still tingled from where his fingers had held her!

'Run over by a steamroller'. Was that really how she looked? Probably, she conceded—it was how she felt too!

'Well?' Nick faced her across the desk, arms folded stubbornly across the width of his chest.

Joey gave a dazed shake of her head. 'I don't even know you—'

'What do you want to know?' he rasped, dark eyes narrowed speculatively. 'I'm thirty-five. Single. Financially independent—believe it or not,' he added smiling wryly. 'And I'm not leaving here until I find out what happened to the spiky, self-confident woman I met here last night!'

Joey stared up at him frustratedly, his sheer size making her very aware of just how small this office really was. 'Nothing happened to me,' she dismissed impatiently.

'Liar,' he murmured reprovingly.

She frowned. 'I do not appreciate being called a liar,' she snapped.

He shrugged unconcernedly. 'Then stop being one,' he advised lightly.

Joey drew in a sharp breath. 'Don't you have work to go to?' she told him pointedly; after all, it was almost ten o'clock.

'Eventually.' He nodded. 'I'm still waiting, Joey,' he reminded her softly several minutes later, the silence between them stretched weightily.

She swallowed hard, totally overwhelmed by this man's persistence. Ordinarily she would have just insisted he leave, but her sleepless night, her worry over David

Banning's presence in England, meant that her defences weren't as firmly in place as they usually were. In fact, she felt quite tearful.

She didn't just *feel* tearful, Joey realised as the tears began to fall hotly down her cheeks!

'I thought so.' Nick nodded, moving quickly round the desk to pull her up into his arms. 'Poor baby,' he murmured softly against her hair as he cradled her against the hard warmth of his chest.

'I'm hardly that,' she choked tearfully, devastated by her emotional breakdown. Maybe if Nick hadn't been so kind to her... 'This is ridiculous,' she decided self-disgustedly, pushing away from him. '*I'm* ridiculous,' she muttered, smoothing back the silkiness of her hair; it was preferable to meeting the concern in those dark brown eyes.

'It's nothing to feel ashamed of,' Nick rebuked gently. 'We all cry sometimes.'

Most people cried sometimes, Joey inwardly conceded. Although somehow she doubted that David Banning ever did; there was a hard steeliness about him that made him a more formidable force than his brother had ever been. Daniel had just ignored or laughed off anything he found unacceptable in his silver-spoon life. Things like having a daughter...

'I'm not ashamed,' she returned, back under control now. 'But, as you can see, the salon is rather busy this morning—'

'Have lunch with me?' Nick cut in determinedly.

Joey almost laughed at the incongruity of the suggestion; lunch with a building labourer, and dinner with a powerful American banker. Could the two men be any more different? Although she knew which one she preferred!

'Haven't you missed enough work already for one day?'

she reasoned. 'Even though you don't work for Dominic Mason, I'm sure your boss can't be this understanding!'

Nick shrugged unconcernedly. 'I do more than my fair share of work,' he dismissed. 'Lunch, Joey,' he said again. 'You look as if you need a break from here. And something to eat might do you some good too,' he added grimly.

It probably would; she had been too upset to do more than drink a cup of coffee before leaving the house this morning. But did she want to have lunch with this man? A man whose touch she could still feel, minutes later, tingling up the length of her arm...?

One look at his determinedly set face told her that she really didn't have a lot of choice about it, that Nick wouldn't leave here until he had her agreement to meet him for lunch.

She sighed heavily. 'There's a sandwich bar just down the road. I'll meet you in there at one o'clock.'

'A sandwich bar,' he repeated drily. 'Can't we do better than that?'

They probably could. But, like her, he probably had a pretty tight budget—especially after his 'heavy date' the evening before! Besides, the way she felt at the moment, she wouldn't do justice to more than a sandwich.

'I only have an hour for lunch; a sandwich will be fine,' she insisted.

'Non-negotiable, hmm,' he realised knowingly.

'Non-negotiable.' Joey agreed with a brief smile.

'Then it will have to do.' Nick nodded. 'One o'clock. Don't be late, or I'll come looking for you,' he warned in parting.

Joey stared after him, wondering how on earth she had got herself into this situation. One minute the man had been a written-off bad debt, and the next she found herself with a date to meet him for lunch!

She had thought yesterday was a bad day, but this one didn't look as if it was going to be any better!

CHAPTER THREE

'COME on, Joey, choose a sandwich,' Nick encouraged smilingly as she continued to study the menu, despite the hovering waitress. 'The government doesn't take this long to make a decision!'

The problem was, she didn't feel like eating anything. As the morning had progressed the hollow feeling in the pit of her stomach had deepened—and it had nothing to do with hunger. Being forced into meeting this man for lunch was guaranteed not to improve that hollowness.

After Nick had gone this morning she had spent at least ten minutes remonstrating with herself for being badgered into having lunch with him at all—although she didn't doubt for a moment that he would carry out his threat to 'come looking for her' if she didn't turn up. His presence at the salon this morning had already created enough speculation, without adding to it.

She closed the menu. 'Just cheese on brown bread. Oh, and a cappuccino,' she told the waitress with a smile.

'It took you ten minutes to decide that?' Nick teased once they were alone again.

Joey didn't know how he had spent the intervening three hours, but he looked just as clean and tidy now as he had at ten o'clock this morning. Not that it mattered to her what he had been doing, she hastily told herself. Except she was starting to become intrigued in spite of herself, was totally aware of everything about Nick...

Which, in the circumstances, was ridiculous. She already had enough to contend with without having to deal with

28

Nick as well. It was amazing, really; there hadn't been a man even on the most distant horizon for over two years, and just when she least needed the complication Nick decided to force his way into her life. Next time a man asked to have his hair cut after hours she would just say the salon was closed and have done with it!

'Is it because you're having to close the salon?' Nick prompted gently.

Joey stopped pleating the tablecloth between agitated fingers, looking up at him. 'Sorry?'

'You're frowning again,' he explained lightly. 'I wondered if your obvious lack of sleep last night was due to worry over relocating your salon?'

She grimaced. 'Amongst other things.'

Although, in all honesty, she hadn't given the problem of the salon another thought after David Banning's visit the evening before. Closing down and relocating the salon paled into insignificance when compared with trying to guess the reason David Banning had come all the way from America to see her. Or, rather, not her; he had obviously come to see Lily. Which was even more worrying.

'Other things?' Nick prompted softly.

Joey gave the slightest beginnings of a smile. 'You're very astute.'

'For a rough and ready building worker,' he added drily.

She gasped. 'I didn't say that—'

'You didn't have to.' He grinned. 'It was there in the surprised tone of your voice.'

'Sorry.' She gave an awkward shrug, totally disarmed by the effect his grin was having on her. In any other circumstances— But, no, she must concentrate on the problem at hand, not create more for herself.

'So tell me what "other things",' Nick encouraged huskily. 'I can keep a secret. Honest,' he added persuasively.

'Most men can,' Joey acknowledged drily. 'It's the one thing they're really good at!'

'Ouch!' Nick winced at her scathing tone. 'I gather from that remark that you've met more than your fair share of male chauvinist pigs? Or is that term out of fashion now?' he added derisively.

She smiled. 'I believe we just refer to them all as selfish bastards nowadays.'

He raised dark brows. 'Not very flattering to their mothers.'

Joey instantly sobered. 'No,' she acknowledged hardly, inwardly wondering whether, when the baby was born, if it had been a boy instead of a girl Daniel would have taken more interest than he had. After all, a boy would have been the Banning heir...

But it was no good wallowing in such conjecture; the baby had been her beautiful, totally adorable Lily, and now Daniel himself was dead, anyway. Without ever having seen his daughter...

She drew in a ragged breath, deliberately meeting the warmth of the enquiring brown gaze across the table from her own. 'I'm a single mother,' she stated flatly.

'Ah,' Nick murmured with a slow nod of his head.

As if he finally had the answer to all his questions, Joey thought bad-temperedly. Which was ridiculous. Dozens of women brought children up on their own these days. For many reasons.

'Ah, nothing,' Joey snapped, leaning back slightly so that the waitress could place their sandwiches and drinks down in front of them. 'Being a single mother has its problems,' she conceded. 'But it also has its benefits,' she added determinedly.

'Such as?' Nick prompted interestedly, before taking a

hungry bite of the club sandwich he had ordered for himself.

'Such as no negative input from an uninterested father!' she bit out with feeling.

Daniel had dealt with the responsibility of having Lily as his daughter with as little trouble to himself as possible: namely he'd paid a set amount of money into a bank account each month.

An amount that had continued to be paid in the four months since he had died, Joey realised slowly. On David Banning's instructions...? If so, why? Daniel's death four months ago had surely completely nullified any responsibility the Banning family might, or might not, feel towards Lily?

'You're frowning again, Joey,' Nick probed softly.

She drew in a ragged breath, at the same time shaking her head in self-derision. It was simply no good tormenting herself with all these thoughts and questions; no doubt she would have the answer to all of them this evening. When she had dinner with David Banning. It was the waiting that was killing her.

'Just ignore me,' she told Nick ruefully, before biting into her own sandwich.

'Oh, I couldn't possibly do that,' Nick told her huskily, his gaze suddenly very intense. 'You intrigue me, Joey,' he added softly.

She stiffened, looking across at him with clear green eyes. 'I wouldn't waste your time, if I were you; I've just told you all that there is to know about me,' she bit out dismissively.

'It's my time to waste.' He shrugged. 'And so far it hasn't been wasted,' he assured her.

Joey found herself mesmerised by the warmth in those deep brown eyes, by the sensual nature implied by that fuller lower lip; she didn't doubt for a moment that Nick would be a caring as well as passionate lover—

Lover? Now she really *had* gone too far!

She put her half-eaten sandwich back down on the plate. 'I have to go—'

'No, you don't,' Nick cut in assuredly. 'I checked in the appointment book earlier while I was waiting in the salon to talk to you; your next appointment—for a perm, I believe,' he added drily, 'isn't until two-thirty.'

He had checked earlier?

Did that mean he had intended inviting her out to lunch all the time? Why else would he have checked the appointment book...?

'Look, Nick, I think you might have misunderstood the situation,' she began hardly.

'Let me see,' he murmured thoughtfully. 'You agreed to cut my hair last night because you had a little time to kill before going home. You didn't believe for one moment that I would return this morning with the money to pay for it, and were obviously surprised when I did,' he continued determinedly as Joey would have spoken. 'You're a single mother. You don't have a lot of time for—or faith in— men. Understandably,' he accepted. 'Have I "misunderstood" anything so far?' He raised mocking brows.

Joey closed her mouth, looking at him with narrowed eyes. No, he seemed to have got the gist of circumstances so far. 'You missed out the fact that I'm not interested in a relationship at the moment,' she finally told him firmly.

'Or at any time in the near future, if I've read the signs correctly,' Nick acknowledged good-humouredly.

Joey glared at him frustratedly. If he had read those signs, what was he doing here?

More to the point, what was she doing here...?

She knew the answer to that only too well; Nick had

read the signs, he had just chosen to ignore them. And he had decided to make her ignore them too.

But not any more. 'Exactly,' she told him determinedly, bending to pick her bag up from the floor. 'Now, if you will excuse me—' She broke off as Nick reached out and took a firm grasp of her arm, looking first at his hand against the paleness of her skin, and then across at the man himself. 'Would you please let me go?' she demanded evenly.

'In a minute.' He nodded abruptly, making no attempt to set her free. 'Joey, don't let one bad experience sour the rest of your life,' he told her huskily.

'*One* bad experience?' she returned mockingly.

'However many there have been,' he dismissed impatiently.

Joey wasn't sure she liked the sound of that! 'Actually, personally, there's only been the one,' she conceded grudgingly. 'But I've seen dozens of other terrible relationships to know it's a lottery out there, and that the man usually has the advantage.' She shook her head. 'I used to say that if I ever ''came back'' I wanted to be a man. But then I gave it a little more thought—and realised that by the time that happened the women would probably be in charge!' She grinned at the thought.

'I think you would get on well with my sister,' Nick said, finally releasing her. 'She is of similar sentiments,' he explained ruefully as Joey sank back down into her chair.

'You have a sister?' Joey asked interestedly. And not just because it would turn the conversation away from her for a while; she was interested in this man in spite of herself!

Nick gave a grin. 'And a mother and father,' he admitted sardonically. 'In fact, I went up to London and had dinner with them all last night,' he added drily, brows arched over teasing brown eyes as he saw Joey's look of surprise. 'Not the "heavy date" you had in mind?' he taunted lightly.

Not exactly, no, she inwardly acknowledged. 'Tell me about them,' she invited softly, relaxing back in her seat now that Nick no longer had that grip on her arm. But, as before, her skin tingled where he had touched her...

'Not a lot to tell, really.' He shrugged. 'My father is something in the City; my mother is the perfect wife and mother. My sister is two years older than me, editor on a newspaper, divorced—and intending to stay that way,' he revealed drily.

Joey gave a rueful smile. 'There's a lot of it about!'

'Unfortunately, yes,' Nick agreed heavily. 'It's a bit tough on us men when all you women have decided that marriage and motherhood aren't for you,' he explained wryly.

Her mouth twisted. 'I've usually found it's the other way round—marriage and fatherhood aren't for you!' she explained as he raised his brows questioningly.

He shrugged. 'Speaking personally—'

'I really do have to go, Nick,' she cut in firmly—she didn't want to know how he 'personally' felt about the subject. Or any subject, for that matter. In fact, the conversation had become altogether too personal for two people who had only met briefly the previous evening! 'I have some shopping to do before my two-thirty appointment,' she added, at the same time taking some money from her bag to pay for her lunch.

'Don't,' Nick warned softly as she would have put the money on the table. 'I think I can manage to pay for a sandwich you haven't eaten,' he added mockingly at her questioning look.

No doubt he could, but it was a fact that most men expected you to pay your own way, even for a sandwich!

'Thank you,' she accepted, putting the money back in bag.

Nick chuckled softly. 'Very graciously done, Joey. Even if it did almost kill you!' he added, still laughing.

Joey returned his smile. 'It was that obvious, was it?'

'I don't know what sort of men you've met in the past, Joey—' Nick shook his head ruefully '—but when I take you out I'll do the paying.'

When he...? But this was a one-off—wasn't it...?

'Don't look so worried, Joey.' Nick reached out and lightly touched her hand as it rested on the table. 'I only want to invite you to have dinner with me this evening.'

The intensity of his gaze easily held hers, and Joey found that her breathing suddenly seemed laboured, her hand once again tingling where he touched her.

What was it about this man that caused her to react in this way? Oh, he was very attractive, ruggedly so, and he could also be extremely charming; that smile could melt even the most hardened of hearts. But even so...

'Don't say no, Joey,' he urged tensely.

She gave a regretful smile. 'I'm afraid I have to. 'I—I already have a date for this evening,' she revealed reluctantly. Her arranged meeting with David Banning this evening couldn't exactly be described as a date, but she didn't know how else to explain it; saying she had to meet the American uncle of her daughter would be revealing too much.

'I see.' Nick abruptly released her hand as he sat back in his chair, his gaze narrowed on her speculatively now.

'I doubt it.' Joey shook her head. 'Would you rather I had said I was washing my hair this evening?' she added impatiently as he continued to look at her in that insulting way.

He shook his head. 'So much for all those brave words on the worthlessness of men!' he scorned.

Her cheeks became flushed. 'I don't believe I actually said that!' she defended heatedly. 'Besides...' she broke off, biting her bottom lip.

There was no way she could explain about David Banning without totally letting her defences down. And she had needed those the last seven years. Needed them still!

'It doesn't matter,' she dismissed briskly as she stood up. 'Thank you for lunch,' she added challengingly.

Nick nodded. 'You're welcome,' he returned tightly.

Leaving Joey with no choice but to walk out of the sandwich bar with as much dignity as she could muster. Which was quite a lot, really. She had needed her pride the last seven years, too!

Another potential romance blown, she accepted ruefully to herself as she wandered around the supermarket picking up something for Lily's tea—not a Mason's supermarket; she refused, as a matter of principle, to use that particular chain of supermarkets!

It was a pity, really, that she and Nick had parted so badly, because she quite liked him—actually, more than liked him. There was a physical awareness between the two of them that was impossible to deny. Although there was no guarantee that it would ever have been any more than that, she argued with herself. Even if she had wanted it to be. Which she probably didn't...

Probably? Get a grip, Joey, she admonished herself. Nick was thirty-five, still single, so what did that tell her about him?

That he just hadn't found the right woman?

Romantic nonsense. The sort of thing she had believed in when she was sixteen years old. Real life wasn't like that. If you were lucky you managed to find someone to share your life with that you were reasonably compatible with; if you were less lucky you managed to live with those differences in uneasy harmony. There simply wasn't a 'right' man or woman in the world for everyone. Mr Right did not exist!

So decided, Joey put Nick firmly from her mind, paid for her purchases and returned to work. She had the much more pressing problem of David Banning to deal with this evening...

She dressed with care for her evening out; a simple black dress that reached her knees, teamed with an emerald-green short jacket that matched the colour of her eyes. It was formal enough for dinner, almost businesslike, in fact. Which was exactly the impression she wanted to give David Banning this evening.

Even from her brief meeting with Daniel's brother the previous evening, Joey knew he was going to be a formidable adversary. Because adversary he most certainly was. When it came to Lily, anyone, or anything, that threatened the even tenure of her carefree young life came under the heading of enemy as far as Joey was concerned. And she had a definite feeling that was exactly what David Banning intended...

'Miss Delaney,' he greeted, standing up smoothly as Joey joined him in the lounge of the hotel at exactly eight o'clock. 'You're looking very nice,' he added evenly.

And God, how it hurt him to say that, Joey observed derisively as she sank down into the chair opposite the one where he was now resuming his own seat. It made her wonder exactly what he had expected the mother of his brother's child to be like. Hard? Grasping? Calculating? She wasn't any of those things. Although he would find

she could be as fierce as a lioness guarding her cub if anyone threatened Lily!

'So do you,' she returned drily.

His clothes might be a little over-the-top for this particular hotel, but there was no denying that David Banning
did the tailored evening suit and white silk shirt justice,
emphasising his broad shoulders, tapered waist and long
legs. The black leather shoes looked as if they might be
handmade too. And why not? The Banning family were
one of the most wealthy in New York.

'The niceties over, I suggest we go in to dinner.' He
stood up, looking down at her coolly with those icy blue
eyes.

Joey stood up too, a humourless smile curving her lips
as she accepted the short duration of those 'niceties'; this
evening was going to be every bit as awful as she had
known it would be.

Although the last thing she had expected to see, as she
preceded David Banning into the hotel dining-room, was
Nick seated across the room at a corner table!

CHAPTER FOUR

WHAT was Nick *doing* here? was Joey's first panicked thought as she sat down abruptly in the chair the waiter held back for her. The chair, while not having its back towards Nick, was sideways on, meaning she could glance across at him if she wanted to.

And Nick could glance up from the papers he appeared to be studying, and see her, too!

Nick looked different tonight, the casual working shirts and denims replaced with a cream shirt and formal trousers. In fact, Joey decided after a brief glance at him from beneath lowered lashes, Nick no longer looked like the approachable workman she had known.

What was he doing, dining at this hotel? And alone, by the look of it; Nick was already on to the main course of his meal, with no sign of a second place ever having been set at the table.

She had assumed that Nick, being part of the construction company working on the new supermarket, would be staying somewhere locally. But she certainly hadn't thought of it being this particular hotel! They must pay building workers higher rates than she had imagined!

'Miss Delaney? Or may I call you Joey now?'

She turned sharply back to David Banning, blinking rapidly as she tried to gather her scattered thoughts together; seeing Nick in this unexpected way had totally unnerved her! 'Of course,' she ceded distractedly, frowning across at her dining companion.

David Banning looked at her quizzically. 'The menu,

Joey,' he prompted. The waiter standing at her side was waiting to hand it to her.

'Oh. Thank you.' She gave the young waiter a brief smile as she took the menu into her shaking hands.

Shaking because of Nick's presence here, she easily acknowledged as she stared sightlessly at the menu open in front of her. Goodness knows, this meeting with Daniel's brother was going to be difficult enough, without the sword of Damocles hanging over her as she waited for Nick to see her here—with the man who was supposedly her 'date' for the evening!

What would Nick do when he finally spotted her—if he spotted her!—seated across the dining-room with the other man? Would he just get up at the end of his own meal and leave the dining-room, too annoyed to speak to her? Or would he come over and say hello?

Until she had told Nick of her prearranged date for this evening she would have said the latter, but his cool reaction to the fact that she was going out with another man made her hope he would do the former. She really didn't feel up to dealing with Nick this evening as well as David Banning!

'Is there something wrong, Joey?'

She looked up to find David Banning looking at her once again with those narrowed blue eyes. As if she were a particularly nasty bug he was studying under a microscope!

Joey closed the menu with a snap. 'You arrived out of the blue last night, informed me that Daniel is dead, and then claimed that the two of us need to talk—of course there's something wrong!' she bit out caustically.

'*Touché,*' he acknowledged drily, slowly closing his own menu to give her his full attention. 'How did you and Daniel meet?'

She stiffened at this frontal attack; the 'niceties' definitely were over! 'At university,' she supplied, as abruptly.

Blond brows rose in surprise. 'At Oxford?'

Joey's mouth twisted derisively. 'Awful, isn't it? The class of person they let in there nowadays if they think they will fit in and they have the right qualifications!'

'Obviously,' David Banning drawled cuttingly. 'Did you know who Daniel was when you met him?'

Joey drew in a sharp breath; obviously this was going to be a 'gloves off' evening. Well, two could play at that game! 'He introduced himself as Daniel Banning,' she returned scathingly. 'I saw no reason to think he might be lying.'

David Banning's face darkened ominously. 'I—' he broke off abruptly as the waiter arrived with the bottle of wine he had ordered, clearly displeased at the interruption even as he tasted the white wine.

Joey breathed an inward sigh of relief at the same interruption. This was turning out worse than she had even imagined it would. Obviously David Banning believed she had been nothing but a gold-digger seven years ago!

Cold, arrogant, pompous...

'What would you like to eat, Joey?' he prompted impatiently, the hovering waiter now obviously waiting to take their order.

Get a grip, Joey, she firmly instructed herself as she gave her order for the soup, followed by Dover sole and a salad; she didn't particularly care what she ate, doubted she was going to taste any of it anyway—the bile rising in her throat at David Banning's condescending scorn would make that impossible!

Well, she refused to be cowed by his attitude. She was thirty years old, for goodness' sake, owned and ran her own business, had been a mother for six years...

But then, that was this man's problem, wasn't it—because she was mother to his brother Daniel's child...?

'Could we just get one thing straight before we go any further with this conversation?' she told David Banning coldly once they were alone again. 'I made no claim on Daniel while he was alive,' she continued at David Banning's reserved nod of acquiescence. 'And I have no intention—'

'I wouldn't call a five-hundred-pound cheque every month, paid into a bank account in your name, making "no claim",' he cut in raspingly.

The colour flooded and then drained from Joey's face, leaving her eyes large and accusing. 'I haven't touched a penny of that money,' she told him from between stiff lips. 'The account you're speaking of is in trust for Lily.'

David Banning raised rueful brows. 'Indeed?'

'Indeed,' she snapped furiously, eyes flashing deeply green.

It had been Daniel's one acknowledgement of the child he had left behind in England when he returned to America at the end of his time at Oxford.

In the circumstances, Joey had been tempted to tell him where he could put his money, but then common sense had kicked in; the money was nothing to do with her, was for Lily's future. Joey hadn't felt she was in a position to make that particular decision for Lily. And so she had reluctantly agreed to have the money paid into an account for Lily's future. A fact David Banning was now twisting around to his own mercenary way of looking at things...

'I can show you the account book, if you would like to see it,' she continued harshly. 'You will find every penny Daniel ever sent—plus interest—is still in there!' It was Lily's money, the very least that Daniel could do for the daughter he had abandoned.

A grudging look of respect briefly crossed David Banning's arrogant features—only to be quickly replaced by his own brand of scathing mockery. 'That won't be necessary,' he drawled.

Because, Joey knew, the money Daniel had given towards Lily's future was nothing but chicken-feed to the Banning family! They were an all-powerful, all-rich banking family in New York, and had been for generations. Whereas the Delaneys had emigrated to England from Ireland only eight years ago, had worked, and worked hard, for everything they had ever had.

'I must say,' David Banning drawled lightly as he picked up his spoon to begin eating the soup that had just been delivered to their table, 'that you aren't at all what I was expecting of the woman who mothered Daniel's child.' He gave her a speculative glance.

'Oh?' Joey guardedly returned that gaze.

'Hmm.' David Banning nodded slowly. 'It came as something of a shock to me when I went through Daniel's things after his death and found the paperwork for the standing order of five hundred pounds to be paid to one Miss J. Delaney every month over the last six years or so—'

'The account is only in my name because Lily was a baby when the payments began,' she cut in sharply. 'If you would let me show you the account details you will see it states quite clearly that it is in trust for Lily—'

'I've already told you I don't want to see the account details.' David Banning dismissed the suggestion with a bored wave of one elegant hand. 'But, as you can probably imagine, at the time of discovery any number of explanations for those cash payments flashed through my mind.'

'I'm sure they did,' Joey acknowledged disdainfully, easily able to imagine what some of those explanations might have been. 'How did you discover the truth?' She frowned.

That question had been bothering her since David Banning arrived outside her home the previous evening. She had known Daniel when they lived at Oxford, but she and Lily now lived hundreds of miles away from there. Deliberately so. Obviously Lily's money was now paid into a local branch of the bank, but that still didn't explain how this man had found out who Lily—and she!—actually were.

Blue eyes met hers unblinkingly. 'Amongst Daniel's belongings I also found some letters. Love letters. From "Josey". At least, I thought it was Josey,' he corrected drily. 'You really should learn to write in a neater hand, Joey,' he drawled pointedly.

Her mouth twisted in the paleness of her face. 'I'll try to bear your advice in mind,' she dismissed. 'OK, so you found…the letters. That still doesn't tell me how you learnt of Lily's existence. Or, indeed, exactly who she is.' She looked steadily at David Banning.

He shrugged those broad shoulders beneath his tailored jacket. 'I hired a private detective—'

'You did what?' Joey gasped incredulously, what little colour there was in her face immediately draining away, huge green eyes dominating the whiteness of her face now.

Just the thought of some faceless, nameless third party digging into the details of her life—without her even being aware of it—gave her a sick feeling in the pit of her stomach.

'How dare you?' she continued angrily, shaking with indignation.

David Banning shrugged again. 'In view of the fact that I live in America—'

'And your time is precious!' Joey put in scathingly.

'—it was the easiest, and most efficient way of finding out exactly what I wanted to know,' he continued as if she hadn't interrupted.

'It was an infringement of my privacy, is what it was!' Joey corrected furiously.

'Perhaps,' he allowed drily. 'I—'

'There's no "perhaps" about it.' Her voice shook with anger, her hands tightly clenched into fists beneath the table.

'I do wish you would calm down, Joey,' David Banning told her in a bored voice.

'I'll just bet you do.' She glared across the table at him, her thoughts racing. Exactly what had this damned private detective found out about her? 'But I have to tell you that I deeply resent having some seedy private detective sifting through the contents of my life—'

'You watch too much television, Joey,' he put in disparagingly. 'The man was quite respectable, I can assure you.'

For respectable Joey instantly read discreet. It really wouldn't do to have the sort of information David Banning had uncovered made public knowledge. How would the Banning family ever be able to lift their heads in New York society again if Lily's existence as Daniel's illegitimate child became public knowledge?

David Banning's gaze was steely now. 'All the man actually turned up was that you run a hairdressing salon. That your private life is non-existent. Obviously he found out your home address,' he revealed mockingly. 'And that you share that home with your six-year-old daughter Lily. In view of those cash payments Daniel paid for the last six years or so,' he continued with distaste, 'it didn't need an Einstein to work out that Lily was the reason for those payments—that she had to be Daniel's daughter.'

'Lily is *my* daughter,' Joey corrected harshly. 'Daniel's so-called payments were just to ease his damned conscience.'

She wished now that she had let her pride win in that situation. Then she would never have been presented with this other—more threatening?—situation.

'What exactly is it that you want, Mr Banning?' she asked guardedly, green gaze hard on the arrogant features across the table.

This man might look like Daniel, but she had quickly learnt that the similarity was only skin-deep. David Banning was hard and shrewd, things Daniel had never been, and Joey also guessed that he could be completely ruthless if the situation necessitated it.

'I'm merely trying—and obviously not succeeding,' he conceded drily, 'to explain my own feelings in this matter.'

Joey eyed him challengingly. 'And are your feelings relevant?' she enquired scathingly.

Blue eyes narrowed coldly. 'If you want those payments to continue being paid into the account—yes!' he rasped harshly.

Her eyes widened on him in puzzlement. 'Actually, I don't give a damn either way about the money. As I told you, it was for Lily. And I'm sure she'll understand when I explain the situation to her when she's older. Besides, you said that Daniel is dead—'

'His obligation to his daughter—unfortunately—is not!' his older brother bit out.

Joey looked at him warily now. Exactly what...?

Her brow cleared as realisation suddenly dawned on her. 'I don't intend trying to claim any of your brother's estate for Lily, if that's what's bothering you!' she told him disparagingly.

Really, did the Bannings think in no other terms but

monetary ones? Money to dismiss an obligation and ease a guilty conscience? Yet more money to dispense with that obligation completely...?

She gave a rueful shake of her head, her expression pitying. 'The chances are I wouldn't even have known of Daniel's death if you hadn't come over here and told me. If the payments had just stopped, for whatever reason, I would have just taken it to mean Daniel considered his obligation settled.'

'I must say,' David Banning began slowly, his steely gaze fixed on her, 'that you don't seem particularly...upset at learning of Daniel's death.'

Of course it was upsetting to learn that a young man of only thirty-two, a man who had so obviously enjoyed life to the full, had died so tragically. But as for anything else...!

She shrugged. 'It was seven years ago,' she pointed out practically. 'My life has moved on a long way since then, and I'm sure his did too.'

Daniel had never been a person for dwelling on or even thinking about the past—or the future either, for that matter! He had lived his life only for the moment. And Joey had been too busy the last six years, trying to provide a settled life for Lily, to give Daniel, or the past, much thought either.

'Nevertheless,' David Banning drawled hardly, 'he was the father of your child—'

'Lily doesn't have a father,' Joey cut in harshly. 'She's never had a father. So if all that's been worrying you is that I might try to take some sort of financial advantage of Daniel's death—'

'It hasn't been worrying me,' David Banning cut in coldly. 'Nothing has been worrying me about this situation,' he added confidently. 'But it is an indisputable fact that Lily is Daniel's daughter.'

Joey stiffened again warily. 'Yes...'

He shrugged broad shoulders. 'Perhaps you aren't aware of the fact that my brother and I were the only children?'

'As far as I was concerned, until your arrival last night, Daniel was an only child!' Joey informed him drily, wondering where on earth this conversation was going now!

He gave a tight smile. 'Well, as you can clearly see, he wasn't,' he rasped coldly. 'Of course, if you had married since Lily's birth this situation would be entirely different,' David Banning continued thoughtfully.

Joey frowned her consternation. 'What situation?'

'The situation of Lily,' he bit out harshly.

'There is no "situation of Lily",' she insisted impatiently. 'I'm her mother. She's my daughter. Those are "indisputable facts", too,' she rasped.

'I accept that.' David Banning gave an abrupt inclination of his head.

'That's big of you,' Joey snapped, wishing someone would take away the bowl of uneaten soup from in front of her; just the smell of it was making her feel nauseous now. As for the rest of the meal...!

He gave her a considering look. 'Were you this fiery seven years ago?'

Joey frowned at his sudden change of subject. 'Probably,' she finally conceded irritably. 'Why?'

David Banning shrugged. 'Only that if you were then it's easy to see the reason for Danny's attraction to you,' he drawled softly, blue eyes admiring now.

Her eyes narrowed, her brow furrowed in a frown. From any other man that remark might have sounded mildly flirtatious. But that was impossible to believe coming from a man like David Banning...

He straightened abruptly—almost as if he had realised that it might have sounded as if he was flirting with her! 'I've told you that Danny and I were the only children, he began harshly. 'Danny didn't marry before his death. And I have no reason to think there might be any more of his illegitimate children out there, either—'

'That must be a relief,' Joey scorned.

'It is,' he agreed sharply. 'Tell me, in this day of easy abortion—'

'My family are Catholics.' She abruptly anticipated his next—insulting!—question.

'Of course,' he accepted smoothly. 'Well, as I said, Danny never married. I was married. Briefly,' he continued raspingly. 'But we're divorced now. And there were no children from the marriage,' he explained harshly.

'There's still plenty of time,' Joey put in quickly, a sickly feeling gathering in the pit of her stomach at the realisation of exactly where this conversation was going!

Daniel had died childless. This man, the only remaining male Banning heir, was also childless. Which made Lily, at this moment in time, as Daniel's only child, David Banning's only successor.

'Unlikely,' he dismissed harshly. 'In the circumstances, I haven't yet told my parents of Lily's existence, I wanted to see her—and you—for myself, before I did that.'

Joey would just bet he had; after all, they might have been completely unacceptable to the Banning family! It afforded her no comfort that David Banning seemed to be coming round to thinking that maybe they would be acceptable after all…!

'You have parents, too? My, what a lot of Bannings there are,' she responded insultingly.

He drew in a harsh breath. 'I'm going to be perfectly frank with you, Joey—'

'I wish that you would!' she cut in uneasily.

His mouth twisted. 'Lily, as Daniel's daughter—'

'Illegitimate daughter,' Joey put in quickly.

David Banning shrugged. 'Under the circumstances that is of little consequence. The fact of the matter is, Lily is a Banning,' he rasped clearly, obviously wanting to make sure there was no room for error in Joey's summing up of the situation.

He needn't have bothered; Joey understood only too clearly what he was saying! Lily, legitimate or not, after David Banning himself, was the only living heir of the Banning family.

She swallowed hard, her lips feeling numb. In fact, all of her felt numb! What was she going to do? Because she had a terrible feeling that David Banning hadn't come over to England just to settle his curiosity about Lily—that, in view of what he had just told her, he was here for a much more ominous reason than that!

'Lily is a Delaney,' she stated firmly. 'And I intend that she will remain so until she marries,' she added determinedly.

David Banning shrugged unconcernedly. 'That, I believe, will be for Lily to decide. When the time comes.'

When what 'time' came? This man, with his underlying ruthlessness, was really starting to scare her!

She opened her mouth to speak...

'Joey,' greeted a smoothly urbane voice. 'What a surprise to see you here.'

She didn't even need to turn to know who that voice belonged to—Nick!

She had to admit that after the initial shock of seeing him here she had completely forgotten about him; her conversation with David Banning had been such that it left no room for anything else!

But the same blinkered concentration obviously couldn't be said for Nick...

She turned slowly to face him, wincing as she saw the sardonic look on his face as he looked at her. Whatever his initial reaction had been to seeing her in the restaurant with the other man, he was now masking it behind an enigmatic smile.

David Banning got slowly to his feet, looking enquiringly at Joey before the coldness of that gaze moved to rest questioningly on Nick.

Joey heaved an inward sigh, knowing she had no choice, in the circumstances, but to introduce the two men! Although the conversation with David Banning was such that she really didn't welcome this interruption!

She stood up herself, feeling at a complete disadvantage seated between the two standing men. 'Nick, this is David Banning.' She deliberately offered no further explanation. 'David, this is Nick—'

'Mason,' Nick put in so smoothly, as he reached out and shook the other man's proffered hand, that the fact that Joey had, until this moment, had no idea what his surname was wasn't in the least obvious.

She frowned. Mason? Nick *Mason*? *Dominic* Mason...? *The* Dominic Mason!

Joey stared at him as if he had suddenly developed two heads. Which, indeed, to her, he had!

The workman Nick was ruggedly attractive and charming, a man she could relate and talk to. Dominic Mason was something else entirely!

Joey shook her head dazedly. She had to be mistaken. The conversation she had been having with David Banning had slightly unhinged her usual calm reasoning. In the circumstances, was that so surprising? But just because Nick's surname happened to be Mason couldn't possibly mean that he...

The challenging look he was now directing down at her said otherwise!

He *was* that Dominic Mason!

Joey swallowed hard. This whole evening was turning out to be a nightmare. The things David Banning had already said to her—and she was sure there was more to come!—were terrifying her. Finding out that Nick—a man she had liked and trusted!—was in fact the 'enemy' she had been fighting for months had shaken much more than that.

Her mouth tightened angrily. She hadn't known who he was the previous evening, but he had certainly known who she was: the female fly in the ointment in the construction of the new Mason supermarket, sitting stubbornly in her hairdressing salon and refusing to budge until her lease came to an end.

Her frown deepened as she remembered their conversation of the evening before, the insulting remarks she had made about Dominic Mason—not knowing at the time that she spoke to the man himself. Not that she could be blamed for that; Nick had known exactly who she was; Joey was the one who had spoken in complete ignorance.

'I thought this was your evening in for washing your hair,' Nick drawled now, raising mocking brows in her direction.

Ha, ha, very funny, Joey's irritated expression clearly told him as she gave him a scathing glance. 'Don't let us keep you,' she told him with sugary sweetness. 'I'm sure, being the busy man you are, that you have somewhere else you have to go,' she added challengingly. 'I'm sure you've heard of Mason supermarkets, haven't you, David?' After their so recent conversation, it almost choked her to use the man's first name, but at the moment she was feeling attacked from both sides. And she didn't know which man to defend herself from first!

David Banning's brows rose in acknowledgement, a grudging respect entering those pale blue eyes as he looked at the other man. 'You're *that* Mason.' He nodded slowly.

'Actually that's my father, also Dominic Mason,' Nick corrected lightly, with a meaningful glance in Joey's direction. 'But, yes, I'm part of the Mason group.' His voice hardened slightly as he answered David Banning.

'Something in the City', was how Nick had described his father. That 'something' was obviously Dominic Mason of the Mason group. A 'group', not just the supermarkets she had supposed! The fact that Nick was Dominic Mason II did little to dissipate the anger Joey felt towards him for his previous subterfuge.

And what on earth he had been doing dressed like a building labourer the day before, Joey couldn't even begin to guess!

'I had no idea Joey moved in such...exalted circles,' David Banning murmured speculatively.

Colour darkened her cheeks at his tone. In view of what David Banning obviously thought of her past relationship with his brother, it didn't take too much effort to guess the conclusion he had come to concerning her relationship with the younger Dominic Mason!

'Banning...?' Nick responded to the other man coolly, frowning in concentration. 'Would that be the Banning family of New York?' He arched dark brows.

'It would,' David Banning confirmed arrogantly, his smile completely lacking in warmth.

Nick gave Joey a mocking smile. 'Exalted circles, indeed,' he drawled derisively.

Joey wasn't sure which man she wanted to slap across the face first!

How dared the two of them stand here growling challenges at each other—no matter how urbanely!—swapping family pedigrees as if she weren't actually here? Although…if she weren't here, the two of them probably wouldn't be growling at each other at all, would no doubt have talked quite comfortably together, probably even find they had several acquaintances in common. Besides herself, of course!

In fact, she was tempted to leave the two of them to do exactly that, anyway!

Why not? She had nothing more to say to either of them this evening—in fact, she doubted she had anything more to say to either of them, period! She also had no appetite for the food still to be served to their table. And, in all honesty, she had had enough of both of them!

'If you gentlemen will excuse me…?' She cut sharply into their conversation, looking at them both coldly as they turned to her enquiringly. Almost as if they really had forgotten she was here! 'I've decided that tonight would be a good night to wash my hair after all,' she told them scathingly, before turning on her heel and walking swiftly from the crowded dining-room.

She was only delaying her confrontation with David Banning; she knew that. But the delay would give her a chance to gather her defences, possibly to contact a lawyer and find out exactly where the Banning family stood with regard to Lily.

Because as far as Joey was concerned they stood where they had always stood—nowhere!

CHAPTER FIVE

'WHAT do you think you're doing?'

Joey turned from unlocking her car to find Nick Mason standing behind her in the hotel car park. 'What does it look like I'm doing?' She pointedly opened the door on the driver's side in preparation for getting inside.

Nick reached out and grasped her arm. 'Joey—'

'Miss Delaney to you—if you don't mind, *Mr Mason*,' she bit out cuttingly.

He gave an impatient grimace. 'What was I supposed to do last night when you began talking about Dominic Mason as if he were some sort of monster?'

'Own up to the fact that *you're* the monster!' Joey rasped accusingly. 'Rather than stand by and let me make a complete fool of myself!' Because she did feel foolish—was also having to completely rethink her feelings towards this man. And she didn't know what they were yet!

'You didn't make a fool of yourself.' He shook his head firmly. 'You simply stated how you felt about the situation. Which, in the circumstances, was perfectly understandable. But you also have to believe that I had no intentions when I came into the salon last night of anything more than a haircut. As for the ''monster'' part, I believe my father has that particular privilege,' he acknowledged ruefully. 'Which is a little unfortunate, because he's actually a very charming man,' he said drily.

Joey shrugged. 'Dominic Mason Senior, or Dominic Mason Junior; they're both the same to me. Now, if you wouldn't mind releasing me; I would like to go home.' She looked down to where his fingers showed up starkly against the green of her jacket.

'I have to disagree with you about either the "senior" *or* the "junior" Dominic Mason being a monster,' Nick rasped impatiently. 'But we'll get back to that later. What—?'

'We won't "get back" to it at all!' Joey's eyes flashed deeply green. 'In fact, we won't get back to anything— after this evening it's doubtful our paths will ever cross again.' After all, they didn't exactly move in the same social circles, did they?

Nick's eyes narrowed to thoughtful slits. 'What was going on in there this evening, between you and your boyfriend?' He nodded in the direction of the hotel behind them.

'David Banning is not my boyfriend!' she spluttered protestingly.

Oh, no doubt David Banning was attractive, in an arrogantly assured way, but he was also made out of stone. Besides, there was a very good—obvious—reason why Joey would never find herself attracted to him!

'Then what was he saying to frighten the hell out of you?' Nick Mason rasped.

Joey stiffened defensively, her gaze wary now. Had she looked frightened? And, if she had, had David Banning seen that fear...? 'I don't know what you mean,' she answered guardedly.

'You know exactly what I mean,' he rebuked gently. 'I had been watching the conversation between you and Banning for over ten minutes before I finally came over to your table; you very obviously didn't like what the man was saying to you at all,' he added shrewdly.

Her mouth twisted. 'In other words, you're saying you came over to rescue me?'

Nick's face flushed angrily at her obvious scorn. 'Is that so hard to believe?'

She shook her head. 'You can't possibly know how I felt just from looking at the two of us.'

'Can't I?' Nick murmured slowly. 'What were the two of you talking about, Joey?'

She knew he had deliberately ignored her request that he address her more formally in future, but now was not the moment to pursue that particular subject. The man was probing too closely into something that was much more important to her!

'You're imagining things—'

'I haven't imagined the fact that you walked out on the man in the middle of dinner,' he pointed out reasoningly. 'Nor did I imagine that look of fear on your face just before I interrupted the two of you. Was he threatening you, Joey?' Nick pursued relentlessly. 'Because if he was—'

'You—and your father—are the only ones threatening me, Mr Mason,' she told him forcefully.

What bothered her most at the moment was that David Banning might have seen her fear. In the circumstances, she might have every reason to feel frightened, but she would rather Daniel's brother hadn't seen how she felt.

'How long have you known Banning?' Nick tried a different approach.

'Long enough,' she assured him with feeling.

Twenty-four hours. It was just twenty-four hours since David Banning had appeared outside her home. But in that short time he had managed to shake the very foundations of her life with Lily.

Nick slowly released her, but his gaze remained intent on the paleness of her face. 'Who is he?' he finally murmured softly.

'I told you, his name is David Banning,' Joey dismissed

impatiently. 'You seemed to know of the family when I introduced the two of you,' she reminded drily.

She wanted to go home. Wanted to go inside, lock the door, barricade the windows, and pray for the Grosvenor Hotel to be struck by lightning! Not that she wished any harm to the other people working or staying at the hotel— not even Nick!—but if the lightning could strike David Banning's room in particular then she wouldn't complain.

'I'm not talking about his name, Joey,' Nick answered her irritably. 'I know that part of it. I want to know what role he plays in your life,' he added grimly.

'Really?' Joey scorned. 'And what makes you think you have the right to ask?'

Nick seemed to relax with effort, forcing himself to do so, his smile rueful. 'How about one cup of coffee and a cheese sandwich…?' He quirked self-derisive brows.

'Half a cup of coffee, and half a cheese sandwich,' Joey corrected with a sigh. 'Look, Nick, please don't think I'm not grateful for your concern—'

'But stay out of it,' he finished drily.

In the last six years, through Lily's babyhood, infancy and now school life, there had been no one, apart from Hilary, for Joey to share her troubles with. And even Hilary didn't know everything. Joey had always known, and accepted, that that was the only way the life she had chosen for herself could ever be. Even more so now.

'Yes,' she confirmed huskily, swallowing hard.

Nick tilted his head cajolingly to one side. 'Have you forgiven me yet for being the dreaded Dominic Mason? Or at least one of them?'

Had she? She still felt rather a fool for the things she had said in ignorance of his identity, but, for the main part, knowing exactly who he was really changed nothing. Especially now…

'What on earth were you doing dressed in the way you were yesterday?' She frowned. After all, it was the reason she had assumed he was just a workman.

Nick grimaced. 'My father runs the business side of things; I like to take a more active role. Believe it or not, I enjoy the building rather than the running of the company.' He shrugged. 'Forgiven me yet?' he prompted beguilingly.

'It doesn't matter,' she said heavily. And meant it. What did it matter who or what this man was, when she had the much more immediate threat of David Banning to contend with? 'But I'm still not moving from the salon until I have to,' she added determinedly.

Nick grimaced. 'Did anyone ask you to?'

'Not recently,' she allowed ruefully. 'I really do have to get home now, Nick. Babysitter,' she added pointedly.

'Hmm,' Nick acknowledged thoughtfully. 'If I was to invite you to have dinner with me tomorrow evening—'

'I would have to say no,' she interrupted shortly. 'So please don't ask.'

He sighed. 'OK, I won't ask you to have dinner with me. How about lunch—?'

'No, Nick.' She couldn't help but smile at his persistence.

Nick returned the smile. 'Why not?'

She shook her head. 'It just wouldn't be a good idea at the moment.' She already had far too much to deal with, without the complication of this man. Besides, he was far too astute; it wouldn't take him long, on closer acquaintance, to work out exactly who and what David Banning was. And she needed to work out how she was going to deal with that problem herself before anyone else became aware of it. If anyone did!

'Does that mean that if I was to invite you some other time I might get a more favourable response?' he teased.

'You're very persistent!' Joey gave a broken laugh.

Nick took a step forward, very close to her now. 'It's a family trait,' he murmured huskily. 'Probably one of our better ones,' he allowed self-derisively. 'Joey...!'

Quite how she came to be in Nick's arms, being gently kissed by him, Joey had no idea!

But it was so long since she had been kissed by anyone other than Lily. So long since she had felt this safe and warm, wrapped protectively in arms that promised to keep her that way. If she ever had...!

The blood was pounding loudly in her ears, her body responding as it curved into his, her lips open to his full possession.

'Joey...!' Nick broke the kiss to rest his damp forehead against hers, his hands cradling each side of her face.

What was she doing? Exactly what she had told herself she mustn't do, came the immediate answer. Wasn't it enough that she had David Banning upsetting things, without bringing in the added complication of Nick Mason?

'That was a mistake,' she told him huskily, swallowing hard, moving gently but determinedly out of his arms. 'Goodnight, Nick,' she added abruptly.

He looked at her frowningly as she moved to get inside her car. 'Persistence isn't the only family trait.' He spoke gruffly before she had a chance to shut the car door behind her.

Joey looked up at him warily. 'Oh?'

'Don't worry,' Nick drawled. 'You'll have plenty of time to find out all the others!'

Joey had no chance to reply to what sounded very much like a threat of intent to her, as Nick slammed the car door closed for her, stepping back to allow her the room to drive away.

Which she very quickly did, her thoughts immediately returning to David Banning. She knew as they did so that Nick was the least of her troubles at the moment!

For one thing, she very much doubted David Banning was going to appreciate the fact that she had walked out on him this evening. But, under the circumstances, to have stayed and eaten the rest of her dinner would have choked her.

She went straight up to Lily's bedroom once the baby-sitter had gone home. Her daughter was fast asleep, blonde hair spread out over her Barbie pillow, the duvet, as usual, having slipped off her long-limbed body as she slept.

Joey reached out and gently folded its warmth about Lily's leggy frame before sitting down in the rocking-chair that stood beside the bed, her heart filled with the fierce love she always felt when she looked at her beautiful daughter.

She loved Lily with the completeness one could only feel towards a child—had taken one look at Lily when she was born and instantly fallen in love with her. That love had only increased over the years.

Nothing, and no one, was ever going to part them!

David Banning hadn't actually said this evening that Lily belonged with the Banning family in New York, but the underlying threat had been there none the less. It was up to Joey to make sure he didn't succeed in those plans. In whatever way she could.

The Banning family might be rich and powerful, might feel they had more to offer Lily than she, as a single working mother, might have, but that simply wasn't true in terms of love and caring. There was no way she would ever give her child up to the Banning family.

Oh, Joey didn't doubt for a moment that the Bannings—David Banning, in particular—had the ways and means of taking Lily from her if that was what they'd set out to do, but she would do everything—and anything—in her own power to stop them doing that. Anything!

In the meantime, she knew she hadn't scored many points with David Banning after the way she had walked out on him this evening. She doubted that happened to him very often!

But to have stayed would have simply prolonged her own misery. And she *was* miserable, allowing the tears to fall now that she was alone with her daughter in the privacy of the home they shared. The only home Lily had ever known. The only home she was ever going to know!

She would not give up her daughter, Joey vowed fiercely in the darkness as the tears fell hotly down her cheeks. It was inhuman, cruel to both Lily and Joey, to even think of parting them.

Joey vowed there and then, as she looked at the innocent beauty of her sleeping daughter, that she would fight the Bannings in any way she could.

'You only delayed the inevitable by leaving so abruptly last night, you know, Joey,' David Banning advised confidently as he stood in the doorway of her tiny office at the salon, wearing a dark grey formal suit with a white shirt and grey tie.

'Would you come inside and shut the door behind you?' Joey asked him icily.

She had not had a good morning so far, and this man's arrival here at the salon was guaranteed to make it even worse. She certainly wasn't in the mood to verbally fence with this man within earshot of her staff and clients!

'Thank you,' she added frostily as, with a taunting smile, he complied with her request.

Although Joey wasn't sure that was such a good idea either, when she realised just how much his height and arrogant bearing suddenly dominated the tiny room!

'And to answer your statement, Mr Banning—' she stood up behind her desk so that she felt at less of a disadvantage '—nothing about our acquaintance is "inevitable",' she told him with a firmness she hoped was convincing.

He arched mocking blond brows. 'I thought we had at least reached the David stage last night,' he taunted sardonically.

Only because she had had no choice but to introduce him to Nick Mason, and it would have looked rather odd if she had continued to address him so formally in front of the other man.

'I believe I would prefer to keep things between us on a formal level,' she bit out coolly.

'As you wish.' He gave an abrupt inclination of his head, sitting on the edge of her tiny desk. 'I did call in earlier, but your assistant said you had to go out unexpectedly...?' he added casually, his brows raised questioningly.

Joey felt the colour warm her cheeks, sure this man had guessed exactly where she had gone so 'unexpectedly'.

The first thing she had done this morning was telephone a lawyer, making an appointment to see him immediately. As far as Joey was concerned, the meeting had not gone well.

'As you can see, I'm here now,' she parried challengingly.

He nodded. 'Is Lily in school today?'

Joey bristled at his casual mention of her daughter. 'She usually is on a Wednesday,' she answered stiffly.

David Banning nodded again. 'I would like to meet her—'

'No!' Joey cut in sharply.

'No…?' he repeated softly. Dangerously so.

She swallowed hard, determined not to be intimidated by this man. Even if she didn't exactly feel full of confidence at the moment!

She shook her head. 'It would only confuse her.'

'Joey—Miss Delaney,' he corrected impatiently at her narrow-eyed look. 'Lily and I will have to meet some time.'

She felt as if the blood in her veins were turning to ice! 'Why?' she demanded huskily.

'I am her uncle,' he rasped.

'So?' she challenged.

He sighed at her deliberate obtuseness. 'I'm sure I made myself more than clear last night.'

She shrugged dismissively. 'Not particularly.'

David Banning gave her a scathing glance. 'Then why did you leave so abruptly?' he drawled. 'Unless…' He frowned darkly, no longer quite so relaxed as he sat on the side of her desk. 'Exactly where does Dominic Mason fit into all this?' He studied her with narrowed eyes.

'Fit in?' Joey echoed warily. 'I don't know what you mean.' She shook her head.

'Your decision to leave last night was made almost as soon as Mason joined us.' David Banning spoke thoughtfully. 'He didn't say too much when he came back inside, after saying goodnight to you, but—'

'Nick spoke to you after I left last night?' Joey gasped.

She had to admit that thought had never occurred to her. For obvious reasons. She had only been intent on getting home to Lily. But Nick had spoken to David Banning again after she left the hotel…?

The older man's mouth twisted wryly. 'He did,' he confirmed drily. 'So, what's the story there?'

'There isn't one,' she snapped. 'At least, not one that I intend confiding to you,' she amended, still concerned with what Nick had said to David Banning 'I— What did Nick say to you?' she broached cautiously.

'Not a lot.' David Banning shrugged unconcernedly. 'He seemed more intent on knowing what *I* had been saying to *you*.'

Joey would just bet he had! She hadn't told Nick what she and David Banning had been talking about so seriously, and so he had tried a different approach; except David Banning, she could easily guess, was even more close-mouthed than she was! In fact, she knew from her own guarded conversations with him that he was.

'Which, of course, you didn't tell him,' she guessed accurately.

David Banning's expression darkened. 'I am not in the habit of discussing family issues with complete strangers,' he rasped.

'Family…! You've known of Lily's existence for only a few weeks, and yet you're trying to class her as part of your "family"?' Joey gasped incredulously, the heaviness inside her chest becoming almost unbearable.

David Banning remained completely unmoved by her outburst. 'She's my niece,' he repeated firmly.

'Only by default,' Joey defended. 'Entirely by default,' she added icily as she remembered the months and years she had struggled on alone to keep together what 'family' Lily had. And now this man, with his millions, just walked in here and claimed he had the right of a 'family' member where Lily was concerned. Absolutely—arrogantly—incredible!

He grimaced. 'I can hardly be blamed for the fact that I didn't know of her existence until after Daniel died.'

Which was exactly what the lawyer had pointed out to her this morning, Joey acknowledged with an inward groan, her face paling. As well as the fact that Daniel had contributed to Lily's financial welfare until the time of his death. A responsibility David Banning had continued since that time.

She was already too well aware of all those things!

She drew in a harsh breath. 'Nevertheless—'

'I *am* going to meet Lily, Joey.' David Banning's mouth had tightened forcefully. 'I don't believe I'm being unreasonable in my request,' he added challengingly.

If she had consulted a lawyer then she was damn sure this man would have done so too, before coming to England. And that lawyer would probably have told David Banning exactly what Joey's lawyer had told her this morning: it was in Lily's interests to become acquainted with her American family. And if the problem was to be put in front of a court of law the child's interests were what would come first.

All Joey could see was months, years, of Lily being passed backwards and forwards between herself and the Banning family. And that was totally unacceptable.

Oh, Joey realised that the Bannings were mega-rich, that they could probably provide for Lily materially much better than she could. But they could never love Lily as much as she did!

How could they? Lily was her daughter—and she was a complete stranger to these people! More importantly, they were complete strangers to Lily...

'Perhaps not,' Joey conceded heavily. 'But do you think you're being fair?' She looked at him with accusing eyes.

'Fair…?' David Banning repeated the word slowly, testingly—as if the word were completely alien to him.

Which it probably was, Joey acknowledged. Daniel had always walked through life taking what he wanted, when he wanted, and after meeting his older brother Joey could see why; the Banning family obviously considered there was nothing—and no one—that they couldn't buy with their millions.

Joey felt as if she was losing control of this situation, as if a rug was very slowly being pulled from under her feet!

She straightened determinedly. 'To Lily,' she clarified. 'Daniel was a man of fierce passions, quickly followed by boredom with the conquest,' she remembered bitterly. 'How do I know that after I introduce you to Lily as the uncle she has never even heard of, let alone met, you aren't going to as quickly lose interest in her, leaving her confused and bewildered?' Green eyes were raised challengingly to icy blue.

David Banning's mouth thinned distastefully. 'Because Joey, I am not my brother,' he bit out scathingly. 'Daniel was ten years my junior—the baby of the family, overindulged by all of us,' he recalled. 'The result was a spoilt, irresponsible man.'

Joey looked at him curiously. 'You don't sound as if you liked him very much…?'

David Banning's expression darkened, his eyes glittering dangerously. 'I loved him!' he ground out harshly.

Joey shook her head slowly. 'I loved my father, cried buckets when he died five years ago, but that doesn't mean I liked him. He was too handy with his fists when he'd had a few drinks,' she explained distantly, remembering all too clearly those shouting binges, the relief she had felt on finally leaving home at eighteen; her father had been much easier to love from a distance!

David Banning shrugged. 'Then perhaps you're right. Perhaps there were things I didn't like about Daniel.' He gave a humourless smile. 'In some ways I envied him his complete lack of obligation to everyone and everything,' he revealed. 'At least, I did,' he added hardly. 'Until I realised several weeks ago that the irresponsibility extended to ignoring his own six-year-old daughter!'

Joey stared at him frowningly, an uneasy feeling in the pit of her stomach. The last thing she wanted was to actually start liking this man!

'I do want to meet Lily, Joey,' David Banning repeated firmly. 'And I think that meeting would be better—for Lily—if it was to come through you,' he added softly.

In other words he would rather not have to do this through a lawyer, but he would if he was forced to do so!

She swallowed hard, moistening dry lips. 'Just a meeting?'

'Just a meeting,' he confirmed lightly. 'You don't even have to tell her who I am at this stage, if you would prefer not to,' he added drily.

She would prefer that the last two days had never happened at all! But she knew only too well that they had, and that the meeting between Lily and the uncle she had never known was now inevitable.

But David Banning had said one thing last night that had given Joey an idea of how to stop this situation from going any further than that. If she had the nerve to go through with it...!

CHAPTER SIX

'WHAT a coincidence; I've just been to the salon looking for you, only to discover it's half-day closing on a Wednesday!'

Joey turned at the sound of Nick Mason's cheerful greeting as he entered the hotel, noting distractedly that he was dressed more formally today, in a dark suit, cream shirt and blue tie; obviously he didn't spend all his time messing about on building sites!

There was no smile on her own lips as she answered him. 'Well, now you've found me.' Just as her courage had been about to desert her. Just as she had been about to give up her wait for Nick to return to the hotel, and leave.

Fate. But was it laughing at her, or was it showing approval of what she had come here to do...? Joey only wished she knew!

Nick reached out and grasped her arms, as if he sensed she was almost in mid-flight, brown eyes studying her closely before he turned to the receptionist. 'Could you arrange for a tray of tea for two to be brought through to the lounge?' he requested lightly, before turning Joey in the direction of the less public room.

'Certainly, Mr Mason.' The pretty redhead was picking up the telephone even as they left.

Joey looked up at him mockingly as the two of them entered the comfortably deserted room that looked out over the hotel gardens. 'So you really are Dominic Mason, after all!' she murmured sardonically. 'You have a certain manner that only comes with complete confidence in who you are,' she explained drily as he raised questioning brows.

Nick shrugged, waiting for Joey to sit down in one of the comfortable floral armchairs before sitting down himself. 'I spend a lot of time in hotels.' He grimaced.

Joey nodded. 'But you're based in London?'

'Most of the time, yes,' he confirmed lightly.

'How much longer do you expect to be here?' she prompted interestedly.

Nick shrugged. 'Another four months or so. On and off. Why?'

Joey stiffened defensively at the suddenness of the question. 'I—I was just making conversation,' she excused, evading that probing brown gaze. 'You said you went to the salon looking for me. Why?'

'Touché, Joey.' Nick smiled, his eyes crinkling warmly. 'I felt our conversation last night was—unfinished.' He spoke slowly, choosing his words carefully.

'Is that why you went back into the hotel and spoke to David Banning?'

Nick's eyes widened. 'So you've seen him again today,' he noted thoughtfully.

Damn, damn, damn; Joey realised, too late, that she was giving Nick information she didn't necessarily wish him to have. She had come here today with the idea of offering Nick a deal. But that deal did not include regaling him with details of her life which were none of his business.

'Briefly,' she dismissed. 'I—'

'Ah, here are our tea things,' Nick said with satisfaction as a waiter placed the laden tray on the table between them before leaving.

As well as a pot of tea, and cups, there were delicate sandwiches and cream cakes on the tray—neither of which,

Joey knew, she would be able to eat. Just the sight of food made her feel queasy at the moment!

In fact, she didn't remember when she had last eaten a meal…

'Eat,' Nick instructed as he seemed to guess her more immediate thoughts, placing a plate before her with two sandwiches on it, before turning his attention to pouring the tea. 'I said eat, Joey,' he ordered again when she didn't move. 'You look as if you're about to keel over,' he added grimly, placing a cup of tea in front of her before adding milk and sugar.

'I don't take sugar,' Joey told him frowningly.

'Today you do,' Nick told her determinedly. 'You need the energy.'

She shook her head. 'Are you always this arrogant?'

'Only when the occasion warrants it,' he answered unrepentantly. 'Drink your tea and eat the sandwiches, and then we'll talk.'

Much as she disliked being treated like a child, the tea actually was very welcome, she discovered after the first sip, even if the unaccustomed sugar did make her wince.

Although perhaps Nick had been right about that, she decided a couple of minutes later as she began to feel slightly better. Not that she intended telling him that, of course; the man was turning out to be arrogant enough already!

'Sandwiches,' he bit out tersely as she would have spoken. 'Or a cream cake, if you would prefer it,' he added mockingly.

'No, thank you.' Joey pulled a face at the thought of eating the sickly sweetness, picking up one of the squares of sandwich to begin nibbling at it uninterestedly.

This had been a terrible idea, she decided belatedly. Born of desperation, yes, but ridiculous, none the less. As she gave Nick a surreptitious glance from beneath lowered lashes—tall, dark, handsome, completely self-assured—she wondered how she could even have thought of it as a possibility. Desperation!

She had lain awake all last night trying to think of some short-term way out of the predicament facing her, until she had come up with an idea she had thought just might work. But today, looking at Nick Mason in the clear light of day, she realised just how much her imagination had run away with her during the night, how unfeasible her night-time solution to the problem really was. If she weren't feeling so desperate, the whole thing would be laughable!

'OK.' Nick put down his cup, watching her from between narrowed lids. 'Tell me what's going on.'

Joey swallowed hard. She didn't even know where to begin! Oh, she knew where the beginning was, she just wasn't sure how much of it she wanted to tell Nick—or, much more likely, how much he would demand to know!

'Or maybe I was mistaken earlier and it's David Banning you came here to see?' Nick rasped at her hesitation.

Joey gave a dismissive snort. 'I've already seen enough of him for one day, thank you very much!' Her hand shook slightly as she placed her empty cup back on the table.

'Why see him at all if you dislike him that much?' Nick queried hardly.

She didn't dislike Banning; in fact, with his admission of a certain jealousy towards his carefree, irresponsible younger brother, he had been almost likeable this morning. No, it was what David Banning stood for, his reason for being here at all, that threw her into complete panic.

A panic that had brought her to Nick Mason with a suggestion he was simply going to laugh at, Joey realised with cringing embarrassment.

'Is he the father?' Nick rasped harshly.

She blinked across at him. 'Sorry…?'

'You told me you have a child; I asked if Banning is the father?' Nick repeated.

'Certainly not,' Joey told him with firm decisiveness.

Nick visibly relaxed, leaning back in his own chair to sip his cooling tea.

As the seconds, and the minutes passed, with Nick just leisurely sipping his tea, Joey's tension began to mount. Why didn't he say something? Anything!

Unless he was waiting for her to speak? But what she had come here to say sounded stupid now. Not just stupid—incredibly fantastic. She should never have—

'My coming here was a mistake,' she told him suddenly, sitting forward tensely. 'I don't know what I was thinking of,' she continued self-consciously, and then gave a shaky laugh. 'I probably wasn't thinking at all!' She shook her head. 'Thanks for the tea, Nick.' She glanced at her wristwatch. 'I really should be going—'

'Not until you've told me the reason you came here,' he cut in firmly. 'Please?' he added persuasively as she raised cool brows at the restraining hand he had put on her arm.

'I came here to offer you a bargain—but I realise now how silly it was,' she dismissed firmly as Nick would have spoken. She gathered up her handbag, effectively dislodging his hand on her arm at the same time. Her thoughts might be filled with the more pressing problem of David Banning, but she hadn't forgotten the fact that Nick had kissed her last night…!

In fact, it was that kiss that had given her the fantastic idea that Nick might be willing to help her…

'Don't you think that's for me to decide?' he prompted softly.

She laughed self-derisively. 'I think I'm quite capable of deciding for myself when I've completely lost the plot!'

She would have to think of some other—sane!—way of dealing with David Banning's avuncular attentions towards Lily.

Nick gave a rueful smile. 'I very much doubt you've done that, Joey.' He shook his head. 'You strike me as a very level-headed, responsible woman—'

'Normally I am,' she agreed unhappily. 'It's just that— the circumstances aren't "normal" at the moment.'

Nick looked at her from between narrowed lids. 'You mentioned offering me some sort of deal...?'

'Yes,' she sighed. 'As if I have anything you would want that badly!' She smiled at her own ridiculousness.

He shrugged, returning the smile. 'Now, that depends on what's on offer,' he said teasingly.

'Not *that*,' Joey assured him drily. 'I was going to offer to vacate the salon immediately in return for—for—well...' She gave an embarrassed grimace.

It sounded even more ridiculous when she tried to put it into words!

'Yes?' Nick prompted curiously.

'Never mind.' Joey shook her head, standing up. 'I really should be going now; I always pick Lily and her friend up from school on Wednesday afternoons.' And gave Hilary the freedom to do some shopping in peace.

'It's only two-thirty, and even I know they don't finish school until at least three,' Nick drawled. 'Sit down, Joey, and let's finish this conversation.'

She frowned. 'I don't remember you being quite this pushy on our first two meetings.'

'My alter ego,' he dismissed unapologetically. 'Would it help if I added another please to my request that you sit down again?' He quirked mocking brows.

'Don't bother.' She shook her head even as she resumed her seat next to him. 'I— You asked if David Banning was

Lily's father.' She couldn't quite look at Nick now. 'And the answer to that is emphatically no—'

'I was having a little trouble believing it anyway,' Nick assured her teasingly.

Joey laughed briefly. 'He's definitely not my type,' she acknowledged ruefully.

'Now, that's interesting,' Nick murmured. 'What would you say is "your type"?'

She shook her head. 'I don't have one. At least, I haven't for several years.' She frowned as she realised the amount of time that had passed since she had even been out on a date. Caught up in being Lily's mother, and her work at the salon, she hadn't even noticed the passing of the years. In fact, the kiss Nick had given her the previous evening was the first in over two years!

'That long.' Nick frowned. 'Any special reason for that?'

Joey gave him an impatient glance. 'None at all,' she answered dismissively. 'Look, we're veering off the subject, Nick,' she admonished impatiently.

He shrugged unconcernedly. 'I was interested, that's all.'

'Well, it isn't relevant to what I'm trying to say,' she snapped. 'David Banning is Lily's uncle. On her father's side,' she explained.

'Obviously,' Nick acknowledged drily. 'So that would make Lily's father—'

'Daniel Banning,' she put in impatiently.

'Hmm,' he murmured thoughtfully.

Joey gave him a searching glance. 'Did you know him?'

'Of him.'

Nick shrugged noncommittally. Although—and it could just be her imagination, again!—Joey felt that he was looking at her speculatively now. Which wasn't so surprising— like David Banning, he was probably wondering how she and Daniel had ever met in the first place!

To her mind, a totally unimportant fact at this particular moment!

'He's dead,' she stated flatly.

Nick gave a slight inclination of his head. 'So I believe. But his family's interest in his daughter is very much alive?' He raised dark, questioning brows.

Joey gasped, rendered momentarily speechless at the astuteness of this man's mind. It had taken her a lot longer than this to realise exactly what David Banning's intentions were, and, as Lily's mother, she had a lot more to lose!

'Yes,' she confirmed huskily. 'I... It appears Lily is the only Banning grandchild.'

'Delaney,' Nick put in evenly.

'My point exactly,' Joey agreed, with relief at his understanding.

He looked at her with narrowed eyes. 'So where do I come into it?'

She sighed. 'You don't. At least...' She hesitated, sighing heavily.

What did she have to lose? Her pride? Not a very high price to pay when compared with the possibility of losing Lily!

She deliberately didn't look at Nick Mason now. 'I... The thing is, I—I need a fiancé! Preferably a rich and powerful one...' she added hardly. 'Someone the Banning family—David Banning, in particular—don't feel they can push around!'

'Me?'

She winced at the mildness of Nick's tone, forcing herself to look at him. But he met her gaze blandly enough, with not a derisive smile or laugh in sight!

She turned away again, swallowing hard. 'It was something David Banning said to me last night...' She drew in a ragged breath. 'The thing is, he said if I had married in the last six years then this situation would be different, that Lily would be in a settled home life, with a mother and a stepfather.' The lawyer she had spoken to this morning had basically told her the same thing! 'Of course, I wouldn't expect you to actually marry me—'

'Of course not,' Nick agreed lightly.

She gave him a reproving frown. 'This isn't in the least funny—'

'I'm not laughing,' he assured her soothingly.

No, despite the fact that she had told him more or less everything, he still wasn't laughing at her...

She sighed. 'All I need to do for the moment is convince David Banning, for the short period of time that he's in England, that Lily does at least have a prospective stepfather—'

'Me.'

'I wish you would stop saying that!' Joey said agitatedly, just the thought of what she was proposing making her irritable.

'Sorry.' He shrugged. 'But what happens when our so-called engagement is called off? When there is no prospective stepfather, rich, powerful, or otherwise...?' he asked drily.

'I'll cross that bridge when I come to it.' She avoided meeting his gaze. 'For the moment, I'm more concerned with dealing with the immediate problem. This morning David Banning asked to meet Lily, and—'

'OK,' Nick said softly.

'—in the circumstances, I had no choice but to... What did you say?' Joey frowned her consternation at his interruption.

'I said OK,' Nick repeated lightly. 'You said you have need of a fiancé.' He shrugged. 'I'll do it.'

Joey stared at him, blinking dazedly. 'You haven't heard what I'm offering in return for your help yet...'

'Immediate vacation of the salon, I believe you said,' he recalled lightly.

He didn't miss much, did he? 'Yes...' She nodded slowly. 'But—'

'The end of next week will do just as well,' Nick assured her. 'I would prefer that we find you somewhere else to move the business to first.'

She gave him a sharp glance. '"We"?'

Nick nodded dismissively. 'After all, it wouldn't look too good to David Banning if my father's company just threw my fiancée—and her business—out onto the street, now, would it?' he reasoned mockingly.

Joey continued to stare at him. Had Nick really just said...? Had he just agreed...?

'Don't you want to think about it first?' She frowned.

'No.' He shook his head.

'But—'

'Joey, any fiancée of mine wouldn't be this indecisive,' he told her drily.

She wouldn't want to be—otherwise this man would simply drive over her like an express train!

Any fiancée of his...

Was it really this simple? She had asked. Nick had agreed. Unquestioningly.

She shook her head dazedly. 'Don't you have...other commitments you need to deal with first?' she asked awkwardly.

His mouth quirked mockingly. 'If you're asking about other women, Joey, then just do it, OK?'

'OK,' she bit out tersely. 'I'm asking,' she snapped.

'Like you, it's been a while.' He shrugged.

Somehow Joey found that hard to believe. Nick was simply too attractive, too forcefully charming not to have a current woman in his life somewhere. But if he didn't want to tell her about that then it was his problem to deal with.

'What time is Banning coming to see Lily this evening?' Nick questioned briskly now.

She frowned at this reminder of the other man. The reason for this subterfuge in the first place! 'I said he could call round at about six-thirty for half an hour, before Lily goes to bed,' she revealed reluctantly.

'Then we don't have any time to lose, do we?' Nick said, standing up. 'I just need to go upstairs and collect a few things first. But I should be with you in about ten minutes.' He nodded his satisfaction with that arrangement.

Joey looked up at him frowningly. 'Where are you going?'

'With you, of course,' he told her confidently.

She stood up abruptly. 'But—'

'Look, Joey.' Nick reached out and grasped the narrowness of her shoulders. 'For this to be in the least convincing it's important that Lily doesn't treat me as much like a stranger as she's going to treat Banning when she meets him later. And for that to happen Lily and I need at least a couple of hours' acquaintance.'

He was right. Of course he was right.

That express train was pulling out of the station.

And still with not a derisive smile or laugh in sight!

CHAPTER SEVEN

'WHAT on earth are you doing?' Joey queried bemusedly as Nick moved about her tiny sitting-room, placing random objects down on the coffee-table and sideboard.

He paused to look across at her as she watched him from the doorway. 'Making it look as if I spend a lot of my time here, of course,' he explained, with the patience of one talking to someone who was slightly simple-minded.

Of course. How silly of her!

'I'm not actually into smoking a pipe, and I don't wear slippers, but these things should do just as well.' He looked at his efforts with satisfaction.

He had placed two books on the side that were definitely not to her taste—a political thriller and a business journal—some CDs of classical music on the coffee-table, and a man's jumper discarded over the back of one of the armchairs. These must be the 'things' he had collected from his hotel room before they'd driven to the school to collect Lily!

'Sorry I asked.' Joey grimaced.

Nick straightened to grin at her. 'Now, now, Joey, no sour grapes just because Lily thinks I'm the best thing since ice cream!'

Amazingly, that was exactly what her daughter thought of this man she had only met for the first time an hour ago. Lily, who was usually quite shy in the company of men—for the obvious reason that ordinarily there were no men in her life!—had taken immediately to Nick, sitting in the car telling him about her day at school, taking him upstairs to show him her bedroom as soon as they reached the house. She would be down from changing into her play clothes in a few minutes...

'I suppose you have a certain charm,' Joey allowed grudgingly.

Nick's smile widened. 'To which you, unfortunately, are completely impervious!'

Not completely, Joey owned inwardly—although she had no intention of letting Nick know that the kiss they had shared last night had affected her more than she cared to admit! In the circumstances they now found themselves in, that would not be a good idea.

She gave him a considering look as he made himself comfortable in one of the armchairs. 'This really is very good of you,' she said slowly, still finding it difficult to believe that he had agreed to help her in this way.

'You can think of a way of thanking me properly later... Just joking, Joey.' He laughed at the stricken look on her face. 'I'm happy to help out. Besides, you have agreed to vacate the salon,' he reminded her. 'Which is going to please my father immensely!'

His father... His family! 'Is any of this—' she indicated his presence in her home '—going to cause...problems for you with your family?'

He raised dark brows. 'In what way?'

Joey pulled a face. 'Well, hopefully this will all be over before anyone else gets to hear about...our arrangement, but—'

'Our engagement, Joey,' Nick corrected pointedly. 'Which reminds me. We had better go and shop for a ring tomorrow—'

'That won't be necessary,' she instantly protested, horrified at the thought.

'Of course it will,' he dismissed. 'We can't have Banning thinking I'm too mean to buy you an engagement ring.'

He had a point, Joey conceded. But… 'You're enjoying this, aren't you…?' she said slowly.

'Something you will quickly learn about me, Joey,' he drawled. 'I very rarely do anything that is going to make me unhappy.'

'That must be nice for you,' she said drily, wondering if she hadn't jumped out of the frying pan into the fire!

But, no, she could put up with Nick's domineering attitude for a while if it meant she managed to deflect the damage David Banning intended causing to the peaceful life she and Lily shared.

'It is,' he confirmed unapologetically. 'So, what are we having for dinner this evening, dear?' He grinned across at her wolfishly.

He wasn't going to 'enjoy' himself that much!

'Roast chicken,' she informed him wryly. 'So if you would like to come through to the kitchen and help me with the vegetables…?' she added pointedly.

'No problem.' He got instantly to his feet. 'I'm a dab hand at peeling potatoes.'

He seemed to be a 'dab hand' at most things, Joey discovered as he dealt with the preparation of all the vegetables while she put the chicken in the oven and laid the table.

'A bachelor has to learn to fend for himself in the kitchen—or starve,' he explained at her surprised glance. 'You—'

'Uncle Nick, would you like to come and play Snakes and Ladders with me?' Lily appeared in the kitchen doorway.

'Go ahead,' Joey invited drily as he shot her a questioning glance.

'OK,' he answered Lily, even as he dried his hands on the towel. 'But I should warn you I was the Snakes and Ladders champion in my family!' He winked at Joey before following Lily through to the sitting-room.

Uncle Nick...

It wasn't a title Joey was particularly happy with her daughter using towards Nick, but, having talked about it on the drive to school, neither of them had been able to come up with a better one. Joey wasn't happy with Lily addressing adults simply by their first names, and their engagement wouldn't look very convincing to David Banning if Lily called Joey's finacé 'Mr Mason'. So 'Uncle Nick' it was.

Joey could hear the two of them arguing good-naturedly over the game as, for the first time ever, she had a chance to cook the dinner while someone else entertained Lily.

Usually she was rushed off her feet—trying to see to the meal, play with Lily, and then do her homework with her. This evening she even had time to sit down, once the vegetables were cooking, and enjoy a peaceful cup of tea.

Don't get too used to this, Joey, she told herself firmly. Nick Mason's presence in their life was only a fleeting one. His normal world was as far removed from her own and Lily's as the Bannings' was!

Her brow darkened as she thought of David Banning. In just over an hour's time he was going to arrive at the house. Would he be convinced by her engagement to Nick, or would he see straight through the ruse for exactly what it was? She sincerely hoped it was the former!

'Wasn't too successful, was it?' David Banning's gaze levelled on Joey as she rejoined him in the sitting-room after putting Lily to bed.

Her daughter had requested that 'Uncle Nick' go upstairs

and read her a bedtime story this evening, leaving Joey briefly alone with David Banning.

His meeting with Lily had been an extremely difficult half an hour. Already besotted with her new Uncle Nick, Lily had obviously been totally bewildered by the arrival of this second 'uncle'. The fact that David Banning was her real uncle had not seemed to impress her at all.

Which wasn't really so surprising. Lily had accepted long ago that there was no daddy in her life; trying to place David Banning as the brother of the father she had never known seemed to be completely beyond her young understanding. It had been a relief to Joey when she could excuse herself and Lily on the pretext of taking Lily up to bed.

Although what the two men had found to talk about during her absence upstairs, she had no idea...

'Exactly what have you told her about Daniel?' David Banning rasped harshly.

Joey stopped her restless pacing of the sitting-room to look across at him incredulously. 'Nothing,' she dismissed drily. 'There was nothing to tell,' she added defensively.

'Nothing to tell...!' David Banning echoed scathingly. 'I disagree—'

'I don't intend arguing with you about this, Mr Banning—'

'It might have helped the awkwardness of the situation if you had managed to call me David in front of Lily!' he put in harshly.

Her eyes widened. 'Don't try and pass the blame on to me for the fact that you're a complete stranger to Lily— David,' she bit out scornfully.

He drew in a deeply controlling breath, his smile, when it came, completely lacking in humour. 'And, like all good mothers, you've warned Lily about talking to "strangers"!' His eyes gleamed coldly.

Her mouth twisted. 'I suppose I should be grateful for he fact that you called me a good mother!'

David Banning shook his head. 'That has yet to be roven—it was merely a figure of speech!'

She drew in a harsh breath. 'You—'

'Could the two of you keep your voices down?' Nick autioned coolly as he came into the room, quietly closing he door behind him as he did so. 'I don't think it's going o help anyone if Lily hears the two of you arguing,' he dded reprovingly.

He was right. Joey knew he was right. But that didn't lter the fact that David Banning had just questioned her bility as a mother. In an effort not to argue with him, she atisfied herself with glaring across at him instead.

'Let's all have a glass of wine and calm things down a it,' Nick suggested smoothly, after looking at their two ngrily set faces. 'I'm afraid I can't offer you anything tronger, Banning; Joey doesn't have any alcohol in the ouse.'

He had been lucky to find a bottle of wine; someone had given it to her for Christmas, and until Nick had started oking around in the cabinet earlier, looking for something o drink with their dinner, Joey had completely forgotten it was there.

But if the immediate future was going to be spent ver-ally fencing with David Banning a glass of wine all round was probably a good idea!

'You know where the glasses are,' she told Nick grate-ully.

In fact, in the short time he had been here before the other man arrived Nick had found out where most of her hings were—in the downstairs of the house, at least. Al-hough it was such a small house—just the sitting-room, itchen and loo downstairs, with two bedrooms and a bath-

room upstairs—that it probably hadn't been too difficult fo
him!

'Fine,' David Banning accepted tersely as Nick looke
at him enquiringly.

'Just hold the hostilities until I return, hmm,' Nick tol
the other man drily before going through to the kitchen.

'He seems very much at home here,' David Banning sai
pointedly.

Joey's cheeks flushed angrily. 'Why shouldn't he be?
she defended, inwardly thanking Nick for his foresight.

David Banning shrugged. 'The two of you didn't seer
particularly...close yesterday evening.'

She looked away. 'No. Well—'

'I'm afraid you'll have to put the blame for that on me,
Nick told the other man smoothly as he came through witl
three glasses of wine already poured. 'I didn't agree wit
Joey having dinner with you on her own.' He handed on
of the glasses to Joey before giving a second one to thei
guest. 'After all, this is a family matter,' he added, befor
sitting down next to Joey on the sofa.

Joey looked at him. She hadn't even given a thought t
the fact that David Banning might have considered thei
behaviour towards each other the previous evening slightl
odd for an engaged couple, let alone considered giving hin
a reason for it. But obviously Nick had...

She gave him a grateful smile before turning back to th
other man. 'In retrospect, I've decided that Nick was right,
she told David Banning challengingly.

He looked completely unperturbed by her obvious insin
uation. 'When do the two of you intend getting married?'

Joey was totally unprepared for the unexpectedness o
the question. Although, in the circumstances, perhaps i
wasn't so unusual...

'Why do you want to know?' Nick was the one to answe

he other man, his arm resting lightly across the back of
he sofa behind Joey as he played with the wisps of hair at
ler nape. 'You surely aren't expecting us to send you an
nvitation to the wedding?' he added mockingly.

'Hardly,' David Banning retorted scornfully. 'I was
merely wondering, if the wedding was imminent, whether
while the two of you are away on your honeymoon might
ιot be as good a time as any for Lily to come to the States
ınd meet that side of her family.'

Joey had been innocently taking a sip of her wine as
Javid Banning spoke, and was so taken aback by his sug-
ςestion that all she could do was splutter ineffectually.

Nick patted her lightly on the back before answering the
ιther man. 'Not possible, I'm afraid,' he responded swiftly.
We wouldn't dream of going anywhere without Lily.'

The other man frowned. 'You would take a six-year-old
ιn honeymoon with you?' He sounded incredulous.

'Not just any six-year-old, no,' Nick drawled. 'But
Lily—yes, of course she will come with us. She and Joey
ιave never been parted,' he added firmly.

Joey didn't know how he knew that, but he was right;
she hadn't been parted from Lily for even a night since she
ιad brought her home from the hospital.

'Besides,' Nick continued firmly, 'if there is to be any
meeting between Lily and her American grandparents Joey
ιnd I would of course want to be present.'

'If…?' David Banning repeated softly.

Nick shrugged. 'I believe it's still in dispute as to
whether or not that would be a good thing for Lily.'

The other man's face darkened angrily. 'They are the
ρarents of Lily's father!' he bit out furiously.

'A father who wanted nothing to do with his own daugh-
er,' Nick came back grimly.

Joey hadn't told him that, either—but again, Nick was

right. Apart from the 'conscience money', she had hear
absolutely nothing from Daniel in the last six years. An
knowing Daniel, he had probably forgotten the reason h
made those payments every month!

'You will find that my parents are not of the same mind'
David Banning stated decisively.

'Perhaps,' Nick conceded hardly. 'But I'm sure I spea
for both of us when I say that Lily will only go to Americ
accompanied by one or both of us.'

He didn't have any choice but to speak for both of the
at the moment. Joey was still recovering from Davi
Banning's suggestion that Lily go to America to meet h
grandparents!

She had realised, with David Banning's appearance her
that he would probably at some time suggest that Lily vis
her grandparents—she just hadn't realised he would wa
that quite so soon. It brought forward all the plans that sh
had barely formed...

'That's fair enough, I suppose,' David Banning allowe
grudgingly.

'"Fair enough"!' Joey repeated incredulously, standin
up restlessly. 'Lily hasn't even been on a plane yet, l
alone travelled anywhere on her own.' She glared down .
the American.

'Joey—'

'You obviously know nothing about children.' She ig
nored Nick's soothing interruption to continue her attac
on David Banning. '"Insensitive" is too mild a word t
describe your suggestion of just taking Lily away from he
and putting her on a plane for five hours, only to be me
at the other end by two total strangers!' Just the thought c
it made Joey go cold all over.

Besides, she had made her bargain with Nick Mason i
order to avoid such a thing happening.

She turned to him. 'Do something!' she snapped.

'I was trying to,' he told her ruefully before turning back to the other man. 'I'm sure such a visit could be arranged— just not yet,' he added firmly.

'And just when do you think such a visit would be…suitable?' David Banning demanded arrogantly.

Nick's eyes narrowed to icy slits. 'When her mother decides that it is,' he grated.

The other man stood up abruptly. 'I can see there's no point in continuing to discuss this any more this evening,' he bit out impatiently. 'But, if possible, I would prefer to keep this out of the hands of the lawyers,' he added softly.

Joey felt herself pale, her hand trembling slightly as she reached up to push the shaggy mane of her hair back over her shoulders, aware that David Banning's last words had been the equivalent of a threat. But it also confirmed for Joey that he was no more anxious for this situation to be made public than she was.

'We'll bear that in mind.' Once again Nick was the one to answer the other man, his own expression speculative.

Because he had also realised David Banning's reluctance to go public with this…?

'Fine,' David Banning snapped. 'I'll be in touch, Joey.'

'We'll look forward to it,' said Nick to the other man, standing up to walk to the front door with him.

Joey sat back down on the sofa once she was alone in the sitting-room, feeling completely drained by the scene that had just taken place. This was going to be much more difficult than she had even imagined.

'Well, that wasn't so bad, was it?' Nick said lightly as he came back into the room.

Joey looked up at him frowningly. Bad—it had been awful!

'It really wasn't, Joey.' Nick smiled across at her, tilting his head searchingly to one side when she didn't respond. 'Banning isn't so sure of his ground as he would like you to think he is,' he assured her softly.

Her frown deepened. 'How do you know that?'

Nick shrugged. 'I may prefer to stay out of the board-room, Joey, but that doesn't mean I manage to do so.' He grimaced. 'I've met men like David Banning before. There's something he isn't telling us,' he added shrewdly.

Joey shook her head heavily. 'Such as?'

'I have no idea. Yet,' Nick continued determinedly. 'But I mean to find out.'

Joey couldn't believe that anything Nick managed to find out about David Banning could possibly make any difference to the outcome of this situation. In fact, it all looked rather hopeless as far as she was concerned.

'Hey,' Nick chided, crossing the room in two long strides. 'Don't cry, Joey,' he soothed as he sat down beside her on the sofa to gather her into the warm strength of his arms.

She hadn't realised she was crying until he'd brought it to her attention, but now she could feel the hot rivulets running down her cheeks, feel their dampness against her face as they soaked into Nick's shirt.

'He just makes me feel so—so helpless,' she choked against Nick's chest. 'As if I no longer have any control over what happens to Lily or myself.' She shook her head desperately.

'I thought that's what you've got me for—to make sure that it doesn't get out of control,' Nick reminded her gently.

It did feel safe in his arms. *She* felt safe in his arms.

But was it all an illusion? Wishful thinking on her part? For the moment it was all she had!

She raised her head, looking at him ruefully even as she wiped the tears impatiently from her cheeks. 'I can't believe

I'm crying again for the second time in two days.' She shook her head self-derisively.

Nick gave her a searching glance. 'Been a while, has it?'

'Six years.' She grimaced.

His brows rose. 'Since Lily was born?'

Joey sighed, straightening slightly away from him. 'I cried for a solid month then,' she recalled shakily. 'I had never felt so alone, so utterly vulnerable. A part of me was angry too, I know now, because I had been left alone with this totally helpless baby. But I finally realised that it was no good crying for someone that I loved but who...who was never coming back.' She swallowed hard. 'They say that acceptance is the hardest part of mourning for someone you love. I can assure you that it's true,' she added ruefully.

Nick moved away from her. 'I see,' he murmured as he stood up.

Joey looked up at him, taking in the suddenly distant expression on his face, realising that he obviously wasn't comfortable dealing with other people's emotional pain. 'I shouldn't have bothered you with that,' she realised self-consciously. 'Thank you for your help this evening. I— It was very kind of you,' she added inadequately.

'Kindness has nothing to do with it,' he rasped. 'We made a bargain, remember?' He shrugged. 'I was merely upholding my end of it.'

Of course. She had forgotten that for a moment. But obviously Nick hadn't—he had just left her in no doubt that it was the only reason he was here!

She would make sure she didn't forget it again. Make sure that moments like the one a few minutes ago, when she had found herself in Nick's arms, didn't happen again, either...

CHAPTER EIGHT

'JOEY, it's that gorgeous man from the other day, here to see you again!' Hilary said breathlessly as she came through to where Joey sat out at the back of the salon eating an early lunch.

Joey didn't need two guesses who it was! And she agreed with Hilary; David Banning was attractive in a remote, sophisticated way, but Nick had a sensuality about him that was irresistible.

Although she was doing her damnedest to do exactly that!

She sighed, putting down her half-eaten sandwich as she stood up to follow Hilary back into the salon. As she had already guessed, Nick Mason stood there waiting for her, once again wearing a formal suit with a shirt and tie. And indeed looking gorgeous!

But, as he had reminded Joey all too forcefully last night, they had a business arrangement, nothing else...

'Nick,' she greeted him coolly. 'What can I do for you?'

'Get your jacket and come out with me,' he returned in as businesslike a tone.

Joey frowned. 'I'm afraid I can't do that just now.' She shook her head. 'My next appointment arrives in ten minutes. In fact, I was just grabbing a bite to eat before she arrived.'

He raised dark brows. 'We have some shopping to do today—remember?'

'Shopping...?' She looked puzzled.

'Yes—shopping,' he drawled mockingly.

Her cheeks felt warm as she finally realised he was referring to their so-called 'engagement ring.' 'I really don't have the time right now, Nick,' she told him awkwardly. 'Besides...' She held out her left hand pointedly, a ring sparkling on the third finger.

Nick took her hand in his, looking down at the ring. 'It's glass.' He finally passed judgement on the solitaire ring, dropping her hand again as he did so.

'Of course it's glass,' Joey returned disgruntledly.

She really wished David Banning and Nick Mason would choose somewhere other than her salon to have these personal discussions; she wasn't comfortable providing entertainment for her customers and staff.

'I could never afford the real thing,' she told Nick scathingly, moving over to the reception desk in an effort to put a little distance between herself and her customers. In the circumstances, it was better than nothing!

As for the dress ring, she had found it in her jewellery box and thought it perfectly adequate for the purpose. Obviously Nick didn't agree with her!

'But I can. As Banning very well knows,' he added pointedly. 'So would you just get your coat?'

'I—'

'A bargain is a bargain, Joey.' He cut across her continued protests. 'And I intend keeping my side of it,' he added determinedly.

'I'll keep my side of it too,' she snapped defensively. 'In fact...' she lowered her voice so that only Nick could hear her '...I've already contacted an estate agent enquiring about property to rent in the town.' A fact—one of them—she would like to keep from her staff until she had everything settled.

'I told you I would help you to find somewhere else,' Nick rasped irritably.

Joey had no idea what was wrong with him today; his previous good humour certainly seemed to have deserted him! But she had no intention of being bullied—by him or anyone else.

'I'm quite capable of taking care of it myself, thank you,' she told him coolly. 'And, if you're really serious about this—shopping—'

'I am,' he assured her grimly.

She sighed her impatience with his insistence. Nick really was taking this thing too far. All she had wanted to do was convince David Banning of Lily's happiness so that he would go back to the States and leave them alone; she really didn't see why she needed to wear an engagement ring to do that.

'Then come back at two-thirty,' she told him exasperatedly, checking the appointment book on the desk in front of her. 'I have half an hour free then.'

'Unfortunately I have a meeting with the architect at two-fifteen,' he rejected.

'Then the...subject will just have to wait, won't it?' Joey snapped.

'I doubt that Banning is going to.' Nick frowned. 'Have you heard from him today?'

She grimaced. 'Not yet.' But she quite expected to; David Banning didn't seem to have any more patience about getting what he wanted than Nick did. Maybe that was what happened when you were so rich you could buy or do anything you wanted. She should be so lucky!

Nick nodded. 'In that case I'll come round to the house later this evening—'

'That really isn't necessary,' Joey cut in quickly. 'I'm sure you're a busy man, and—'

'Tell me, Joey,' he said thoughtfully, 'does David Banning look anything like his younger brother?'

She gave him a startled look. What on earth...?

'There's a superficial likeness, yes.' She nodded frowningly, remembering her shock two evenings ago when David Banning had first got out of the car; for a few brief moments she had thought it was Daniel.

'I see.' Nick nodded slowly.

'What?' Joey frowned her frustration. 'I don't—' She broke off as the bell rang over the door and a customer came into the salon. Her next client, as it happened... 'Sorry, Nick.' She grimaced. 'But I really do have to go now.'

'As I said, I'll come to the house later this evening.' He turned abruptly on his heel and left.

Even as Joey greeted her customer with her usual friendliness, and draped a protective robe around her, Joey's thoughts were elsewhere.

From having a life completely free of males, she now had two of them constantly interrupting things. And what a pair they were. She wasn't sure which of them she found the most baffling!

'Well?' Hilary prompted with eager interest later that afternoon, before she prepared to leave and collect the two girls from school. It was the first free moment the two women had had to talk to each other.

'Don't ask!' Joey shook her head self-derisively. 'Just remind me the next time I start moaning about life being all work and no play that it's much less complicated that way!'

'I wouldn't mind a "complication" like those two!' Her friend laughed—a tiny redhead, her gamine features covered in freckles.

'Oh, you would,' Joey assured her drily. 'Believe me, you would!'

Hilary grinned. 'If you get fed up with one of them—either of them—just pass him on to me!'

'I wouldn't do that to such a good friend,' Joey countered.

Hilary laughed again. 'See you later.' She gave a brief wave before hurrying off to the school.

By five-thirty Joey was exhausted. And not just because it had been a busy day at the salon. David Banning hadn't telephoned or called in, which was worrying. As for Nick...! She had no idea what was wrong with him today.

A couple of hours' fun with Lily, followed by a long soak in a scented bath, sounded like a good idea to Joey. In fact, it sounded like a wonderful idea. It was never going to happen, of course. Joey knew that. But it was nice to daydream sometimes!

She knew her surmise was correct when she stopped the car outside the house and found David Banning's hire car already parked there, and the man himself on the garden wall waiting for them.

A slightly different-looking David Banning from the one Joey was used to...

The dark blue T-shirt and blue denims, as well as showing his lean masculinity to advantage, somehow made him look younger and more approachable.

But maybe that was the idea...?

'I thought you were going to call before coming here again?' Joey got out of her car to snap her displeasure at his second unexpected appearance, literally on her doorstep.

He shrugged unconcernedly, sliding down off the wall onto the pavement in front of her. 'Good evening, Joey,' he greeted her pointedly at her own lack of manners. 'And good evening to you too, young lady.' He turned to smile at Lily as Joey held the back door of the car open for her daughter to get out.

GET FREE BOOKS and a FREE GIFT WHEN YOU PLAY THE...

Lucky 7

Just scratch off the silver box with a coin. Then check below to see the gifts you get!

SLOT MACHINE GAME!

YES! I have scratched off the silver box. Please send me the 2 free Harlequin Romance® books and gift for which I qualify. I understand I am under no obligation to purchase any books, as explained on the back of this card.

386 HDL DRM7

186 HDL DRNP
(H-R-10/02)

FIRST NAME

LAST NAME

ADDRESS

APT.#

CITY

STATE/PROV.

ZIP/POSTAL CODE

7	7	7	**Worth** TWO FREE BOOKS **plus a** BONUS **Mystery Gift!**
🍒	🍒	🍒	**Worth** TWO FREE BOOKS!
♣	♣	♣	**Worth** ONE FREE BOOK!
🔔	🔔	🍒	**TRY AGAIN!**

Visit us online at
www.eHarlequin.com

Offer limited to one per household and not valid to current Harlequin Romance® subscribers. All orders subject to approval.

© 2000 HARLEQUIN ENTERPRISES LTD. ® and TM are trademarks owned by Harlequin Enterprises Ltd.

The Harlequin Reader Service® — Here's how it works:

Accepting your 2 free books and gift places you under no obligation to buy anything. You may keep the books and gift and return the shipping statement marked "cancel." If you do not cancel, about a month later we'll send you 6 additional novels and bill you just $3.34 each in the U.S., or $3.80 each in Canada, plus 25¢ shipping & handling per book and applicable taxes if any.* That's the complete price and — compared to cover prices of $3.99 each in the U.S. and $4.50 each in Canada — it's quite a bargain! You may cancel at any time, but if you choose to continue, every month we'll send you 6 more books, which you may either purchase at the discount price or return to us and cancel your subscription.

*Terms and prices subject to change without notice. Sales tax applicable in N.Y. Canadian residents will be charged applicable provincial taxes and GST.

If offer card is missing write to: Harlequin Reader Service, 3010 Walden Ave., P.O. Box 1867, Buffalo NY 14240-1867

BUSINESS REPLY MAIL
FIRST-CLASS MAIL   PERMIT NO. 717-003   BUFFALO, NY

POSTAGE WILL BE PAID BY ADDRESSEE

HARLEQUIN READER SERVICE
3010 WALDEN AVE
PO BOX 1867
BUFFALO NY 14240-9952

NO POSTAGE
NECESSARY
IF MAILED
IN THE
UNITED STATES

'Hello, Uncle David,' Lily responded shyly.

He turned to pick up a gaily wrapped parcel from the wall behind him. 'This is for you.' He held the present out to Lily.

Joey gave a nod of consent as Lily looked up at her uncertainly, biting back her own resentment at the gift. If David Banning thought that he could come here and buy her daughter...!

'Thank you.' Lily gave him a shy smile, her face lighting up with pleasure as she opened the parcel to discover the doll that she had already pleaded with Joey to ask Father Christmas to get for her the following Christmas.

A lot of Lily's friends already had the doll, but it was very expensive. Lily had small toys bought for her between her birthday and Christmas, but it was a tacit agreement that the bigger toys had to wait for the more important anniversary of Christmas.

'Isn't that lovely, Lily?' Joey enthused warmly as she went down on her haunches beside her daughter. 'Now we won't have to ask Father Christmas for it after all,' she added lightly.

Lily looked totally overwhelmed by the enormity of the gift. 'Do you think Father Christmas will mind?'

Joey smiled confidently. 'Of course not.' She would just have to go into the toy shop where she had the doll on order and tell them she no longer needed it!

Lily smiled again at her uncle. 'Thank you.'

'You're welcome.' David Banning returned her smile.

Joey straightened, unnerved by the sudden likeness she had seen between the two, her heart sinking as she looked at them. For years she had thought Lily bore no resemblance to her father, but, seeing her face to face with David Banning, Daniel's older brother, Joey knew she had been wrong...

'Shall we go into the house?' she suggested sharply, sure that her neighbours, friendly though they all were, had noticed the comings and goings of David Banning and Nick Mason to her home the last few days!

'I was wondering if I could take you two ladies out to dinner this evening,' David Banning proffered as he followed them inside.

Joey turned from hanging up Lily's school bag. 'That's very kind of you, but—'

'There's a great burger restaurant in town I thought Lily might like,' he neatly cut across Joey.

Her polite refusal was to have been on the grounds that it would be too much on a school day for Lily to go out to a formal restaurant to eat—a fact he had just neatly taken care of with his suggested eating place! It also happened to be one of Lily's favourite places...

'Oh, can we, Mummy?' Her daughter looked up at her with pleading green eyes.

How could she possibly say no when Lily looked at her so endearingly? She couldn't. A fact she was sure David Banning had been counting on!

Joey looked at him coldly. 'If you wouldn't mind waiting in the sitting-room while we go upstairs and change?' She glared her displeasure with his machinations.

'Fine,' he accepted easily.

This was all happening too fast, Joey worried as she helped Lily choose some clothes to go out in. Between caring for Lily, going to work, fending off visits from David Banning and Nick Mason, she wasn't getting a lot of time to formulate her own plans for the future. Plans that didn't include either of those two men!

'You look beautiful,' David Banning complimented lightly when they joined him downstairs a few minutes later, immediately putting down the newspaper he had been glancing through as he sat in the armchair waiting for them. 'Both of you,' he added huskily.

Joey frowned across at him. What was he up to now? That last remark had sounded almost flirtatious. Besides, denims and a fitted T-shirt, although suitable wear for a burger restaurant, were not exactly glamorous...

'We'll meet you at the restaurant,' Joey told him as she picked up her car keys, having no intention of driving back into town with him; that would mean he'd have to come back to the house with them later.

David gave her a narrow-eyed look, but made no demur at the suggestion. 'Fine.' He held the front door open for them to precede him.

'He's nice, isn't he, Mummy?' Lily remarked innocently as they began their drive.

'Yes, he is,' Joey agreed through gritted teeth.

Bribery and corruption, it appeared, did work with a child as young and impressionable as Lily! Not that Joey could exactly blame her daughter; David was being deliberately charming this evening. Besides, as far as Lily was concerned her own mother accepted this man's sudden appearance in their lives.

Joey could have cried with frustration at the situation she found herself in, feeling as if she was slowly sinking under the weight of it all.

The Banning family could so obviously offer Lily a better life materially than she ever could. Lily, if accepted by them, would have the best of everything—meet people, go places, have a lifestyle that Joey could only dream of giving her. Was she wrong to deny her daughter those things?

Stop it, Joey, she instantly ordered herself firmly. If she didn't believe the drastic action she was shortly going to take was the best thing for Lily, then what possible chance did she have of succeeding?

She was Lily's mother. The only family her daughter had known in all her six years of life. She loved Lily and Lily loved her. She refused to accept that the Bannings could ever love Lily as much as she did.

But they could give Lily other things, came that traitorous voice once again, things that Lily, with maturity, would perhaps value much more than the love of her mother, well-intended as it might have been.

Oh, God, this was awful! She couldn't bear the thought of the hole that would be left in her life if Lily only visited her American family, let alone contemplate...contemplate—

'Are you all right, Mummy?'

She glanced briefly at a frowning Lily, realising she had to stop this if she didn't want to upset her daughter. 'Of course I am, darling.' She smiled brightly. 'This is an unexpected treat, isn't it?' she added lightly as she parked the car next to David Banning's outside the restaurant.

Lily made no attempt to get out of the car, giving Joey a quizzical look. 'Do you like Uncle David?'

Out of the mouths of babes and innocents...!

She drew in a deep breath before answering. 'I don't really know him well enough yet to know whether I do or I don't,' she answered honestly. 'How about you?'

Lily shrugged. 'Well...he did give me the doll, and I shouldn't be ungrateful.' She hugged the doll to her. 'But I think I like Uncle Nick better,' she added candidly.

Nick!

Joey had forgotten all about him in the surprise of finding David Banning waiting for her when she got home. Well...'forgotten' was too strong a word, Joey acknowledged ruefully; he wasn't a man it was easy to forget! She just hadn't given him a thought once she'd arrived home and found David Banning there. What on earth was Nick going to think when he arrived at the house, as he had said he would, and found they had gone out? What would he say when he realised it was David Banning they had gone out with?

Because Nick *would* say something; she already knew him well enough to realise he had something to say on most subjects!

'She really is the most beautiful child,' David Banning remarked softly at Joey's side as the two of them watched Lily while she ran excitedly about the restaurant's play area during the wait for their food to be delivered to their table.

'Yes,' Joey agreed guardedly.

'Very like her mother, in fact,' David drawled as he turned back to look at Joey.

She stiffened warily. Apparently David wasn't only being deliberately charming to Lily this evening!

'You know,' David continued, his gaze easily holding hers as he watched her intently, 'it really is a pity that you're engaged to marry Mason.'

Joey frowned. Wasn't David the one who had said it would be better for Lily if she had a father as well as a mother? She would never have thought of offering Nick that bargain if he hadn't!

'I don't understand.' She shook her head dazedly.

David shrugged. 'Well, it's obvious to me that the thought of Lily being involved in what you see as some sort of emotional tug-of-war is very distressing for you...'

Distressing? It was much more than that!

It was inconceivable to Joey that the Banning family should take this interest in Lily after all these years. Not just inconceivable—it was pushing her towards a course of action that threatened to spiral all of their lives out of control.

'Did you ever expect it would be anything else?' she

returned flatly, distractedly watching Lily as she played so innocently on the slide and climbing frame, completely unaware of the war that was already raging around her—and about her.

David shrugged again. 'I hadn't even given a thought, until meeting you, to how you would feel about any of this.'

Joey turned to look at him, green gaze unflinching. 'What do you mean?'

He grimaced. 'You aren't at all what I expected of one of Daniel's girlfriends.'

Joey bristled resentfully. Not because of the use of the word 'girlfriends'; Daniel hadn't ever been the type of man who would be without a woman in his life for very long. It was the implication behind David Banning's words that she somehow didn't fit into that type that she resented.

'And just what did you "expect"?' she challenged hardly.

David shook his head ruefully. 'I think, in the circumstances, it might be better if I didn't answer that! I would like to say, though,' he continued as Joey would have spoken, 'that I have been more than pleasantly surprised.'

Which didn't say a lot for what he had expected to find when he came looking for Lily and herself!

'And?' she snapped.

He grimaced again. 'Now, I have to admit, I'm in somewhat of a quandary.'

Joey shook her head. 'I don't see why.'

David sighed. 'The facts, as I saw them on paper—'

'On paper!' Joey repeated scathingly. 'Lily and I aren't facts on a piece of paper. We're human beings! More than that, we're mother and daughter!' she added angrily.

'Yes,' he recognised evenly, absently playing with the fork at his place-setting. 'I have to admit, once I had realised exactly who Lily must be, the reality of your feelings as her mother hadn't really occurred to me until after I arrived here and saw the two of you together.'

Joey's eyes narrowed. 'You aren't making much sense.' She frowned.

How could he not have taken a mother's feelings towards her child into consideration? Perhaps the fact that he was childless himself went a long way to answering the question. Although not completely...

'Probably not,' he acknowledged with self-derisive hardness, sitting back abruptly. 'My brother died. Suddenly. Unexpectedly. And while sorting out his personal papers I discovered certain...documents that led me to the conclusion that Daniel had a daughter I had hitherto known nothing about—'

'He biologically fathered a child,' Joey cut in forcefully. 'There is a difference.'

'I see that now.' David nodded, his expression grim. 'Damn it, it all seemed so cut and dried before I came over here and met both of you!' He shook his head self-disgustedly.

A bubble of hope was starting to build up inside Joey. Maybe, just maybe, this might all come right, after all...

'As I said earlier,' David rasped, 'it's a pity you're going to marry Mason.'

Joey frowned her consternation. 'I still don't understand why.' She shook her head in complete confusion.

David gave a humourless smile. 'Because, my dear Joey, if you weren't engaged to Mason, don't you see that the most sensible solution to the dilemma we find ourselves in would be for the two of *us* to marry!'

Joey stared at him.

Mainly because, at the moment, she couldn't do anything else; he had just rendered her completely speechless!

The two of *them* to marry? People didn't marry each

other for such clinical reasons as the securing of custody of a child—did they...?

Why not? came the immediate answer; she had asked Nick to enter into a bogus engagement with her for the very same reason!

But that was different. She instantly defended her own actions. She had done what she had as a means of preventing this other man trying to take Lily away from her.

But now he was offering her an alternative to her own drastic course of action...

'I am serious about this, Joey,' David continued, intently watching the shocked stillness of her face. 'I'm unmarried. And so are you. Lily is a Banning,' he added hardly. 'A fact that could be legalised as soon as you became my wife. The only stumbling block that I can see to the two of us marrying is how you feel about Mason.' He raised blond brows.

How she felt about Nick?

This man couldn't know it, but she hardly knew Nick. Their engagement was a fabrication. But could she really contemplate marrying David Banning instead, a man she knew even less about?

'Think about it, Joey,' David encouraged as he saw Lily returning, reaching across the table to give Joey's hand an encouraging squeeze before releasing it and turning his attention to the happily excited Lily.

Think about it, David had said—Joey had a feeling she was going to be able to do little else!

CHAPTER NINE

PARKING her car outside the house a couple of hours later, and seeing Nick's pick-up already parked there, Joey knew she wouldn't have to wait long to hear exactly what he thought of her and Lily spending most of the evening with David Banning!

And after the traumatic couple of hours she had just spent with the other man she didn't think she was up to it. That bubble of hope she had so briefly experienced had been rent asunder rather than just burst!

How could she possibly marry David Banning?

Nick, wearing faded blue denims and a navy-blue shirt, got slowly out of the pick-up as Joey and Lily approached the front door of the house, his gaze narrowed censoriously.

'Nick,' Joey greeted him lightly as he walked over to join them.

His expression was grim as he nodded to her in greeting before looking down at the sleepy Lily. 'Hello, pumpkin. New doll?' he asked interestedly.

He didn't miss a thing, did he? Joey berated inwardly as she unlocked the door to let them all into the house. A fact she would do well to remember, she was sure...

'Uncle David gave her to me,' Lily answered him smilingly.

'She's beautiful,' Nick told her admiringly. 'Have you had a nice evening?'

'Yes, thank you,' Lily had time to answer before giving a huge yawn.

'Time for bed, young lady,' Joey cut in firmly, avoiding

looking directly at Nick, although she was very aware of the animosity emanating from him. 'Would you like to make yourself a coffee or something while I take Lily upstairs?' she suggested hurriedly.

'Or something,' he muttered in agreement.

Joey ignored his obviously angry tone, trailing wearily up the stairs after a sleepy Lily, knowing Nick would be out of luck if he expected to find any more wine to drink; the three of them had finished off the bottle last night, and she didn't have any more in the house. But maybe by the time she came back downstairs Nick would be feeling less annoyed.

Or, conversely, more so…!

For the moment Joey didn't care, just glad of the respite, and still having trouble believing the last couple of hours she had spent with David Banning. The man had as good as asked her to marry him!

Absolutely incredible!

How on earth had the man gone from arrogant hostility directly to a marriage proposal?

Joey gave a shake of her head as she helped the tired Lily into her nightclothes before tucking her up in bed, her new doll at her side. Of course.

Not that Joey had had the opportunity of giving any sort of answer to David's incredible suggestion—Lily and the food had arrived at the table before Joey could recover from the shock of what he had just said to her, putting an end to any more private conversation between the two adults.

Which wasn't to say Joey hadn't given David Banning a few frowningly thoughtful looks from beneath lowered lashes when she'd known he wasn't looking at her.

He hadn't looked as if he'd had some sort of brainstorm since she'd seen him last night. And yet she could have no doubt that he wasn't quite sane to have made the suggestion he had.

Less sane than she had been when she made a similar suggestion to Nick Mason? she again reminded herself...

But that was different, she instantly defended. Her bargain with Nick was for expediency only, and very short-term, whereas what David was suggesting was much more long-term than that.

Oh, Joey had no illusions as to the reason he had said what he had. She knew that his only motive was to officially bring Lily into the Banning family. It was just so ironic that David Banning should make such a suggestion when marriage was something Daniel had never even considered as an option seven years ago.

Joey knew she had never felt so tired in her life—emotionally tired—as she did walking back down the stairs to see Nick. And knowing this evening was far from over.

How had all of this happened?

Four days ago her life had been going steadily along, as it had for the last six years, the only blot on her horizon the fact that she had to find new premises for her hairdressing salon. Now she found her future with Lily seriously under threat—the only way out of it seeming to be to agree to vacate the salon in a week's time in exchange for Nick Mason's agreement to a bogus engagement. And now, on top of all that, David Banning had suggested the two of *them* should get married!

No wonder she was tired!

Nick stood up as she entered the sitting-room, his gaze narrowed searchingly on the paleness of her face. 'What's happened?' he questioned intently.

Joey gave a weak smile; trust Nick to realise that something had happened!

'Has Banning been threatening you again?' Nick probed astutely.

She might not feel so disorientated if he had; at least it would have been in character. What had actually happened certainly couldn't be called that!

'Not exactly,' she replied heavily. 'Actually, it was quite a pleasant evening.' Even to her own ears she sounded surprised about that fact.

Apart—apart!—from David's suggestion that the solution to the problem would be for the two of them to marry, it had been a pleasant evening. David, with his change to less formal clothes, seemed to have changed in other ways too—teasing Lily, charming Joey, making both of them laugh on several occasions. In fact, as the evening had progressed, Joey had begun to wonder if she might not have misjudged him.

It couldn't have been easy for him to come to England to meet his niece and her mother for the first time. Lily, at six, wasn't that difficult to come to terms with, but he couldn't have known what to expect of Lily's mother— especially as the only thing he really knew about her was the evidence of those bank payments. Could Joey really blame him for the conclusions he had come to—?

What was she doing? One evening together when David had set out to be deliberately charming did not nullify the other occasions he had insulted her and as good as threatened her!

'A "pleasant evening",' Nick repeated sceptically.

'Well, it was,' Joey returned defensively.

'Hmm,' Nick murmured thoughtfully. 'In that case, why has David Banning decided to be nice, after all...?'

Because he had decided the most obvious answer to this dilemma was for Joey to marry him!

Although somehow Joey knew she wasn't going to tell Nick about that...

Maybe she had been slightly precipitate in entering into this bogus engagement with Nick, but until she got to know David Banning a little better it was probably wise to leave things exactly as they were.

She wasn't seriously considering David's suggestion—was she...?

Think about it, David had told her. Well, she had—she still was—and, so far, the only objection she had found to accepting his proposal was that she didn't love him.

The only objection...!

But was loving the person you married really so important? She had already reached the age of thirty without finding a man she could love and want to be with for the rest of her life, so why should she think that might change in the next ten or fifteen years? The chances were that it wouldn't. And if she married David there would be no bitter wrangle over custody of Lily; Lily would simply become the Banning that David wanted, that she really was. In fact, Lily's life would be transformed.

When Joey looked at the situation logically like this the fact that she and David didn't even remotely love each other didn't seem particularly relevant...

'Joey?' Nick prompted at her continued silence.

She snapped her attention back to the more immediate problem, smiling brightly at Nick. 'You don't seem to have made yourself a cup of coffee or anything, after all; would you like me to make you one now?'

'I would like you to answer my question,' he returned doggedly.

She shook her head. 'I'm afraid it isn't one I'm qualified to answer.' She turned towards the kitchen. 'Maybe you should ask David,' she hedged.

'So it's David now, is it?' Nick murmured ruefully as he followed her to lean back against one of the kitchen units.

'He is Lily's uncle.' Joey shrugged, avoided meeting that melting brown gaze, though Nick looked at her probingly as she moved deftly about the kitchen making their coffee.

'I believe we can accept that as fact,' Nick accepted grudgingly. 'But other than that you know nothing about the man.'

Joey turned to give him a teasing smile. 'I don't know much about you, either,' she reminded him lightly. 'And we appear to be engaged to each other!'

'Exactly,' he said with satisfaction. 'Which reminds me...' He reached into his pocket. 'I have something for you.'

When she saw the ring box he'd produced Joey had to put down the two cups of coffee she had been holding; her hands were shaking so much she was in danger of spilling the hot liquid all over herself!

She swallowed hard. 'Nick—'

'Don't say anything until you've looked at it,' he said huskily, flipping up the lid of the box to hold it out in front of her. 'If you don't like it we can go back to the shop and change it.'

Not like it! As Joey looked down into the open box she knew it was the most beautiful ring she had ever seen in her life; a huge emerald surrounded by six slightly smaller diamonds. She also knew, in the circumstances, that she could never wear such a ring.

She wiped suddenly damp hands down the sides of her denims, shaking her head. 'I can't accept that—'

'Of course you can,' he countered briskly, taking the ring out of the box to pick up her left hand and slide the ring onto her third finger.

Joey stared at the ring, tears springing unbidden into her

eyes; she really had never seen anything so beautiful. The emerald glowed deeply green, the diamonds surrounding it glittering mesmerisingly.

'I chose the emerald because it's the same colour as your eyes,' Nick told her.

Joey looked up at him, but the tears made it difficult for her to focus on his face.

'Joey…!' he murmured throatily, seconds before his head lowered and his mouth claimed hers.

She had been denying this attraction to herself from the moment she first looked at this man, had told herself that the only thing between them now was a business arrangement. At the first touch of Nick's lips against hers she knew she had only been fooling herself…!

Her heart leapt in her chest, her body curving instinctively into his even as she responded to his kiss, her arms moving up over the broadness of his shoulders, her fingers becoming entangled in the dark thickness of the hair at his nape even as his mouth moved in slow, sensuous exploration against hers.

Her lips parted beneath his as the kiss deepened and lengthened, their breath warm, Nick's arms so tight about her now it seemed he might snap her slenderness in two.

But the hard feel of Nick's body against hers was completely pleasurable, his chest muscled, his stomach firm and flat, thighs hard with desire.

'God, Joey…!' He finally broke the kiss to breathe raggedly, the dampness of his forehead resting against hers as he still held her tightly against him, his eyes closed as he fought for control.

Joey could barely breathe herself, her body warm and aching, wanting—wanting—

She moved abruptly away from him, and Nick's arms dropped to his sides as he felt her resistance, his brown eyes warm as chocolate as he looked down at her searchingly.

Joey turned away, unable to withstand that piercing gaze, her breathing ragged, shocked to the core of her being at the desire that still held her in its thrall. Her desire for Nick had been instant, overwhelming, and her body was still shaking with longing.

'Joey?' Nick had moved close behind her, his hands reaching out to grasp her shoulders.

She stiffened, swallowing hard, not knowing what to say. Not knowing if she could say anything! Her voice might not actually work if she tried to speak.

Earlier this evening she had reviewed her situation logically, had already half decided that marrying David Banning wouldn't be such a bad thing, that Lily—whose welfare was, after all, the most important thing in all of this—would be saved so much heartache if Joey was to accept David's proposal. But Joey's response to Nick just now made a mockery of that logic!

How could she think of marrying anyone—for whatever reason—when she could respond to Nick in the way that she just had?

'I'm sorry, Joey.' Nick spoke gently behind her, his hands falling away from the stiffness of her shoulders. 'That went a little further than I had intended. Put it down to the fact that it isn't every day I become engaged,' he added gruffly as she still made no reply.

She drew in a harsh breath, almost afraid to turn and look at him. Afraid she would want to move straight back into his arms!

She closed her eyes, moving determinedly, her chin raised defensively as she finally turned to look at him. Her chest ached at how handsome he looked standing there, his own face flushed with recent arousal, brown eyes darkly caressing as he looked back at her.

Something she had to stop. Right now! 'That wasn't a very good idea, was it?' she eventually managed, turning to pick up the two cups of coffee before marching through to the sitting-room.

Nick wasn't behind her when she turned from putting the cups down on the low table that stood in front of the sofa. Where was he?

More to the point, what did he now think of her, after the passionate kisses they had shared? Because, although Nick seemed to be taking the blame for what had just happened, Joey was well aware of the fact that she had responded to those kisses. Very aware!

Every inch of her straightened defensively as Nick finally strode into the sitting-room, his own expression guarded now as he bent down to pick up his coffee.

Joey could feel her very nerve-endings screaming as the silence stretched and grew between them. One of them would have to say something. Eventually. Wouldn't they...?

'He may look like Daniel, Joey,' Nick finally rasped into the tense silence. 'But he isn't him!' he added harshly.

She knew exactly who he was talking about—but she had no idea what relevance David's likeness to Daniel had to anything. 'I'm well aware of that...' She frowned across at Nick.

His eyes narrowed, a nerve pulsing in the tightness of his jaw. 'Are you?'

'Of course,' she dismissed waspishly. 'Why wouldn't I be?'

Nick shrugged. 'You tell me. Because you certainly don't seem quite so averse to the man as you were two days ago!' he added harshly.

She shook her head impatiently. 'I have no idea what you're talking about.'

'Don't you?'

'No,' she snapped irritably. 'If only for Lily's sake it has to be better if—'

'Yes, that's the question, isn't it?' Nick cut in sharply. 'Just how far are you willing to go "for Lily's sake"?'

Joey froze. What did he mean? Could he possibly have guessed at the solution to the problem that David had put forward this evening? Of course he couldn't, Joey instantly answered herself. But, given time, he just might...

She looked at Nick defiantly. 'I believe that is for me to decide—don't you?' she challenged disdainfully.

'That depends,' Nick drawled slowly.

Her cheeks coloured angrily. 'On what?'

He shrugged. 'On any number of things.'

'Such as?' she prompted impatiently, the desire she had known in this man's arms a few minutes ago having now been replaced by anger.

The two of them had a deal, and, despite what might have happened between them just now, it was a purely business arrangement. And, like Nick, she was keeping to her side of it by vacating the salon. Whatever else she did in her life she felt was none of this man's business!

Nick looked at her consideringly, a smile playing about his lips as he studied her. 'Tell me, Joey,' he finally said huskily, 'have you had much success in putting men off in this way?'

The flush deepened in her cheeks. 'I don't know what you're talking about!'

He shrugged. 'Oh, I think you do,' he drawled gently.

Joey glared at him. 'There haven't been too many men to put off—a ready-made family isn't something too many men are willing to put up with when there are so many single women out there still available!'

'I find that very hard to believe.' He shook his head. 'Lily is adorable. And so is her mother,' he added before Joey could make any sharp reply, brown gaze once again caressingly warm.

She swallowed hard, desperately trying to maintain her own side of that gaze—and failing miserably, as she couldn't withstand the warmth in those dark depths a second longer!

This could not be happening to her!

Under normal circumstances someone like Dominic Mason would never even enter onto the fringes of her life; his business and social connections were well beyond her reach. And she knew he was only in her life now because she had something he wanted and they had made a deal on it.

She knew all of those things, but...

Why did there always have to be a 'but'?

Don't do this to yourself, Joey, she told herself firmly. Her life and Lily's were already complicated enough at the moment without—without—

'I think you had better go,' she told Nick abruptly.

'Do you?' he said softly.

'Yes!' she snapped forcefully.

'OK,' he accepted ruefully.

His acquiescence left her feeling suddenly deflated. And then she remonstrated angrily with herself again, for feeling that way. She had asked him to go; it was ridiculous to feel disappointed because he had agreed to do just that.

'Joey?' He looked at her searchingly. 'What is it?' he prompted at her continued silence.

She forced herself to snap out of her disappointment.

'Nothing,' she bit out dismissively. 'I'll walk you to the door.'

Dark brows quirked mockingly. 'Making sure I leave the premises?' he taunted as he strolled out into the hallway.

'Making sure the door is locked behind you, actually,' Joey corrected impatiently. 'There have been a few robberies in this area in the last few months.' As there seemed to be in most urban areas nowadays!

All humour left Nick's face, his expression darkening as he frowned. 'In that case, I'll listen outside to make sure the door is definitely locked.'

She didn't want him to do that; didn't want him to be concerned about her; didn't want… She didn't want to feel the way she did about him, with part of her not wanting him to leave at all!

'If you feel you must,' she dismissed, even as she pointedly held the front door open for him to leave.

Nick paused in the open doorway. 'I do,' he murmured, reaching out a hand to gently cup one of her creamy cheeks as he gazed down at her intently. 'Everything is going to be fine, Joey. You'll see.'

No, she would not 'see'! And everything was not 'fine'!

How could it be fine? she inwardly choked once Nick had gone, sitting down heavily on the bottom of the stairs, her face buried in her hands.

Hands that felt weighed down by the emerald and diamond engagement ring.

Joey stared down at the ring, the jewels gleaming back at her almost in mockery, it seemed.

David Banning had suggested she marry him and solve this problem neatly and efficiently. And until a few short minutes ago, fantastic as the suggestion might sound, she had been coming round to the idea that it might be a possibility.

But not ten minutes ago she had discovered a very good reason why she couldn't possibly contemplate marrying anyone at this moment in time.

She was falling in love with Nick Mason!

CHAPTER TEN

THERE were bells ringing. Noisily. Persistently.

'What...?' Joey roused herself from sleep, totally disorientated as she looked desperately around her bedroom for the source of that ringing.

At last she found it—the bedside telephone!

Obvious, really, if you thought about it, she acknowledged dazedly, even as she sat up in bed and pushed the tangle of blonde hair out of her face.

Eleven-thirty-six. Her illuminated bedside clock read eleven-thirty-six. Whoever was ringing her at this time of night had better have a very good reason indeed for doing so!

She snatched up the receiver. 'Yes?' she snapped grumpily. If someone wanted to ring at this unsociable time of night they could take the consequences!

'Did I wake you?' Nick's unmistakable voice came back lightly.

Did he...? 'Of course you woke me!' she confirmed impatiently. 'It's eleven-thirty—' she glanced at the bedside clock again '—thirty-seven,' she told him, too disgruntled at being woken up to even begin to think of the confusion his kisses earlier this evening had caused in her.

'You're a bit...bad-tempered when you first wake up, aren't you?' He sounded amused.

Considering she could only have been asleep for thirty minutes or so, was that so surprising?

She had gone straight up to her bedroom after Nick left, but despite reading for a short time to relax her, and determinedly not allowing thoughts of either Nick Mason or David Banning to enter her head, she hadn't been able to fall asleep straight away, tossing and turning beneath the bedclothes before sleep finally claimed her. Consequently, she now felt as tired and confused as she had when she'd first come up to bed!

She sat up straighter in bed. 'How did you get this telephone number?'

'Strangely enough, you're in the local telephone directory, under J. Delaney,' he answered drily.

That didn't mean it was an open invitation to every Tom, Dick…and Nick to just pick up the telephone and call her whenever they felt like it!

'What do you want, Nick?' she prompted irritatedly.

'It occurred to me, once I was back at the hotel, that I hadn't asked when you were seeing Banning again,' he came back blandly.

It had occurred to him…! 'That was over two hours ago,' she pointed out impatiently.

'Yes, well, I thought about it first—'

'And then decided to wake me up to ask a question that could quite easily have waited until the morning!' she cut in forcefully.

'I couldn't sleep,' he returned ruefully.

'Well, obviously I didn't have the same trouble!' she rejoined sarcastically.

'Because you already knew the answer to the question,' Nick came back derisively.

She might know the answer to that particular question, but there were a lot more she had no answer to at all! Nick himself, for example!

Joey sighed. 'David has asked me to have dinner with him tomorrow evening,' she admitted, with a certain amount of reluctance.

There was a brief, telling silence on the other end of the line. 'Just you?' Nick finally bit out abruptly.

'Just me,' she confirmed evenly, her hand tightly gripping the telephone receiver now.

'And?' Nick prompted.

'And I told him I would let him know in the morning,' Joey admitted impatiently.

'When you had discussed it with me,' Nick drawled drily.

She hadn't given Nick a thought at the time—and he knew it, damn him!

Although he could have no idea why her thoughts had been in too much of a turmoil, earlier this evening, to make any logical decision about accepting an invitation to have dinner on her own with David Banning the following day.

'Actually, no,' she told Nick drily. 'I already know what your opinion of the invitation will be!'

'Ah, but do you know the reason why?' he taunted.

'You don't like David. You don't trust him. You question his motives in coming here. Shall I go on?' Joey derided.

'No, I think that pretty well sums up the situation,' Nick drawled ruefully. 'But you could have added that I'm also starting to question your judgement,' he added softly.

She bristled resentfully at the accusation. 'In what way?'

'In every way,' he came back forcefully. 'Joey, don't you realise it costs the man nothing to change tactics and start being charming instead of aggressive? In fact, now that he's actually met you, it's probably all too easy for him to be the former,' he muttered disgustedly.

'"Now that he's met me"?' she echoed in a dangerously soft voice.

'I'm sure I don't have to tell you what a beautiful woman you are, Joey,' Nick began patiently.

'There are a lot of things you don't have to tell me, Nick,' she cut in irritably. 'But I have a feeling that isn't going to stop you!' She settled down against the pillows; if Nick was going to keep her up she might as well be comfortable while he did so!

He sighed. 'You're also vulnerable, Joey. Lily makes you so. A fact Banning is very much aware of,' he added hardly.

'I thought that was where you came in,' she returned mockingly.

'It is. If you would let me,' he continued harshly. 'You've already had dinner alone with Banning once this week, and taken Lily out with him this evening, too; how is it going to make our engagement look if you go out with him on your own again tomorrow evening?'

'As if we're both mature adults. As if we trust each other,' she returned waspishly.

Nick sighed. 'You're missing the point, Joey. Deliberately so—'

'Oh, but I'm not,' she assured him with deceptive lightness. 'And I agree with you. Up to a point.'

'That point being…?' he prompted warily.

'That point being when you try to tell me how I should or shouldn't behave,' Joey snapped, once again sitting up in her bed.

'Our engagement is purely a business arrangement, Nick—or had you forgotten that?' she challenged hardly.

There was another silence on the other end of the line. A silence that unnerved Joey the longer it continued…

'Nick…?' she prompted when she could stand the silence no longer.

'I thought we had both forgotten that earlier this evening.' He finally spoke gruffly.

The hot colour warmed her cheeks as she remembered

all too clearly how earlier—briefly—she had wanted to forget everything but Nick, and the pleasure of being in his arms. Even Lily. Which, as she'd built her life around her daughter for the last six years, shocked her more than anything else could have done...

'It would be better if we didn't forget it again,' she told him tightly.

'Better for who?' he said huskily.

'All of us,' she returned determinedly.

She shouldn't fall in love with this man. Couldn't fall in love with him. To do so would be the height of folly on her part. She could ultimately lose Lily because of it...!

'It wouldn't be better for me, Joey.' Nick spoke softly. 'In fact, just thinking about it is what's stopped me going to sleep tonight!'

She drew in a ragged breath, knowing she must not allow herself to be seduced into loving this man.

'Try counting sheep!' she advised scathingly, before disconnecting the line.

And she placed the receiver beside the telephone rather than back on its cradle...

She didn't want to talk to Nick any more tonight. She dared not talk to him—was already fully aware of the seductiveness of their conversation, with them both lying in their respective beds as they talked to each other. The knowledge drummed up all too vivid pictures of Nick as he lay naked in bed, and she was easily able to imagine that his chest was tanned, and covered lightly with dark brown hair. As for the rest of him...!

She turned over in bed with a self-disgusted groan. These wild imaginings were helping nothing. Solving nothing. In fact, they just served to confuse her more.

Her only consolation was that maybe—just maybe—Nick might now be lying awake, tormented by the same erotic thoughts that she was!

'You look as bad as I feel,' Nick murmured as he looked across the restaurant table at her.

Joey had never eaten out so much in her life as she had the last few days! Although...perhaps 'eaten' was too expansive a description for what she had been doing; she had gone out to a lot of restaurants and ordered food, but she hadn't actually managed to eat very much of it!

'Thanks!' she drily answered Nick.

She hadn't been at all surprised when he'd turned up at the salon half an hour ago with the intention of taking her out for lunch; she knew him well enough by now to know he would want to finish last night's conversation. The one she had ended so abruptly!

As for the way they both looked and felt; she couldn't answer for Nick, but she knew she was extremely pale from lack of sleep the night before, and felt as if she had sawdust under her eyelids, too. Nick—to her eyes—in the casual white shirt and fitted black trousers, just looked more handsome than ever!

Nick gave her a considering look. 'Why did you hang up on me like that last night?'

She gave him an exasperated look. 'Nick, there was nothing you said to me during that call that couldn't have waited until today!'

He arched dark brows. 'No?'

'No!' she snapped. But she didn't like the stillness about him, that air of watchfulness. As if he knew something she didn't...

'Hmm,' he murmured thoughtfully. 'OK,' he dismissed with sudden briskness. 'We'll return to that in a few minutes. What have you done about—?'

'Now, just a minute,' Joey cut in agitatedly. 'What will we "return to in a few minutes"?'

'—Banning's dinner invitation for this evening?' Nick continued, as if she hadn't interrupted. 'You did say you were going to let him know this morning,' he reminded her hardly.

'Nick, I don't think—'

'It's really quite simple, Joey; either you are going out with him this evening or you aren't,' he bit out.

'I'm not!' she snapped impatiently. 'Not that it's any of your business!' she added angrily.

Nick seemed to relax slightly, her answer obviously pleasing him. 'What reason did you give for not going?' His eyes were narrowed speculatively.

Joey's cheeks were flushed with anger at his sheer doggedness. 'Well, I certainly didn't tell him that my "fiancé" is so possessive I'm not allowed out on my own!' she snapped furiously.

'Very funny,' said Nick tersely.

Joey sighed. 'Friday is my late evening at the salon. It also happens to be Lily's evening for swimming club.' She shook her head. 'There simply isn't time to do anything else with the evening once Lily and I get home.'

Once again Nick looked thoughtful. 'In that case, why didn't you just tell Banning that last night?'

Because after David's suggestion that the two of them should marry she hadn't been able to think straight! At the time she hadn't even realised that today was Friday! Although she had no intention of telling Nick that, either...

'I forgot, OK? I simply forgot!' she returned aggressively. 'Is that so unusual, in the circumstances?' she challenged as he looked unconvinced.

'Let's order some lunch,' he decided as the waiter appeared beside their table. 'And I suggest we keep the subject on mutually unprovocative subjects for the duration of the meal,' he added drily. 'That way you may actually stand a chance of eating it! You've lost weight this last week, Joey, and you're so slim already you really can't afford to.' He frowned.

Joey ordered her food—a prawn cocktail followed by a chicken salad—deliberately keeping her attention on the waiter, smiling at him in a friendly way as she gave him her order; after all, it wasn't his fault she was so agitated!

But inside her it was a different matter; she hadn't been aware that Nick had noticed her enough the first time they met to realise she had lost five pounds during the last five days.

But obviously he had. And it was disconcerting, to say the least.

It was probably as well that she hadn't known what was going to happen after that first meeting with this man—because if she had known what was going to follow then she would have told him the salon was closed and suggested he come back in the morning! At which time she would have neatly turned him over to Hilary to have his hair cut.

'Any progress on alternative premises for the salon?' Nick asked conversationally once they were alone again.

Joey shrugged, absently playing with the bread roll on her side-plate. 'Several options, but nothing definite yet.'

'Any of them suitable?'

She looked up at him impatiently. 'Is this your idea of a "mutually unprovocative subject", Nick?' she challenged incredulously. 'Because if it is, I'm afraid I have to disagree. The only reason I have to look at alternative premises at all is because your company has taken over my present ones!'

'Correction, it was your landlord who sold the property to my father's company,' Nick refuted smoothly.

'Isn't that the same—?' Joey broke off abruptly as the waiter returned with their prawn cocktails, placing them carefully in front of them before wishing them a pleasant meal.

A pleasant meal! Joey couldn't remember what that was any more!

'Isn't that the same thing?' She leant across the table to hiss at Nick.

'Not at all,' he dismissed easily. 'Have you thought of taking up one of the units within the supermarket complex itself?' He looked at her interestedly as he spooned some of the prawn cocktail into his mouth.

'At the rents you're asking?' Joey scorned, well aware of the rents being asked by the Mason group for the six units within their complex.

He shrugged. 'I'm sure, in the circumstances, my father would be willing to come to some sort of…reasonable arrangement.'

Joey eyed him suspiciously. 'What circumstances?' she voiced uncertainly.

He surely hadn't told his family of their bogus engagement?

'The fact that we're responsible for the loss of your original premises, of course,' Nick answered lightly. 'What did you think I meant?' He arched dark brows.

What she was thinking was that this man was playing with her, that he knew exactly what she had thought. She just didn't know why…

'I really have no idea,' she said, eating her own prawn cocktail too. But, for all she could taste of it, it might as well have been cardboard she was eating!

'So?' Nick prompted lightly.

'So what?' She shrugged impatiently. 'So I'm not interested in one of those units.'

'Why not?' he persisted.

Her eyes flashed deeply green. 'It's a matter of principle!' Her mouth twisted scathingly. 'I'm sure you know what principles are...?'

'Oh, I know what they are,' he confirmed softly. 'I just don't see where they come into this situation.'

'Never mind.' Joey shook her head, playing with the prawns in her dish. 'Anyway, I'm not in any great hurry to find new premises.' Her head went back challengingly. 'It will be the school holidays soon; I thought I might take Lily away for a few weeks before opening up a new salon.'

Nick arched dark brows. 'Really?'

'Yes, really,' she confirmed defensively.

At once she wished that she hadn't. She sounded just too defensive at the moment.

Nick gave a slight inclination of his head. 'Where were you thinking of going?'

Her mouth thinned. 'As far away from New York as possible!' she answered without hesitation.

'Because the Bannings live in New York.' He nodded understandingly. 'Joey, when I was at your house last night—'

'I thought we weren't going to discuss that!' Her spoon hit her dish with a clatter as she almost dropped it. As it was, she ended up with Marie-Rose sauce all over her hand, and picked up her napkin to wipe it off disgustedly.

His mouth twisted into the grimace of a smile. 'By "that", I presume you mean the fact that we kissed each other?' He shook his head at the telling blush on her previously pale cheeks. 'But I wasn't going to talk about that,' he assured her drily. 'Although that isn't to say I don't think it needs some discussing—'

'Then what was it you were going to say?' Joey rudely cut across his throatily teasing remark.

He leant back in his chair to look across at her consideringly. 'You're very defensive today, Joey,' he said softly. 'More so than usual. Any special reason for that?' he prompted gently.

His gentleness was something Joey could well do without; she was so tensely strung out at the moment she didn't know whether she was going to cry—or laugh hysterically!

She shrugged. 'No more so than there was yesterday.'

'Oh.' He nodded. 'Only I couldn't help noticing when I was at the house last night that there have been a few changes made in your sitting-room and kitchen—'

'So I've been doing a little late spring-cleaning,' Joey derided, suddenly feeling as if her legs were turning to water; this man was altogether too astute—and she had thought she had been so careful, too! 'That isn't a crime, is it?' she challenged, eyes wide.

'Not at all,' he drawled easily. 'In fact, it's commendable. But they weren't the sort of changes I was referring to...'

Joey tensed. She couldn't help it. Despite his air of relaxation, this man was far too sharp. In fact, he was getting far too close altogether...!

'Oh?' she prompted distantly, the sick feeling in the pit of her stomach telling her that this was yet another meal she wasn't going to get through.

'Hmm.' Nick nodded, having no trouble at all finishing his own prawn cocktail. And looking as if he had thoroughly enjoyed it! 'There were several things...missing.' He spoke slowly, carefully, as if weighing the words before saying them.

Joey forced herself to continue looking at him unflinchingly. 'Such as?'

'The box with Lily's toys in—'

'I've moved it up to her bedroom,' she interrupted sharply. 'The sitting-room isn't a very big room anyway.' Her mouth twisted derisively. 'And now that we seem to be having such a lot of visitors—'

'It wasn't just Lily's toys, Joey.' Nick cut softly across her mocking explanation, his gaze darkly penetrating. 'The clock was missing from the fireplace—'

'I knocked it over while I was dusting—'

'—and a photograph that stood on the corner table, of you holding Lily when she was a baby, has also disappeared—'

'I've moved it upstairs into my bedroom,' Joey protested curtly. 'Nick, I really don't see—'

'—and the pictures, stuck on the fridge with magnets, that Lily has obviously brought home from kindergarten and school over the years, have also been taken down,' Nick continued with grim determination.

'So what?' Joey scorned incredulously. 'Really, Nick, I've left your jumper, books and CDs exactly where you put them the other night, so I don't see what you're complaining about.'

But she did; she saw only too well!

As, apparently, did Nick...!

She drew in a sharp breath. 'Tell me, Nick,' she began slowly, her gaze narrowed on him consideringly, 'Exactly why did you telephone me last night? And please don't insult my intelligence by saying it was to ask when I was seeing David again!' Her eyes flashed in warning.

She had sensed earlier that Nick had an air about him that spoke of knowing something he wasn't talking about... She had a feeling she now knew what that something was!

He gave a rueful grimace. 'I'm sure, after this conversation, that you know exactly why I telephoned you last night,' he said drily.

Her mouth set exasperatedly. 'Humour me!'

'OK.' Nick shrugged, with an acknowledging inclination of his head. 'I was merely checking to see that you hadn't already done the disappearing act that you so obviously intend doing—along with Lily, of course—in the very near future!'

Joey stared at him.

Just stared at him.

Because he was absolutely right...

CHAPTER ELEVEN

JOEY shook her head dazedly. She had thought about this situation from every angle—legally, emotionally—and—as Nick seemed to have guessed all too easily!—had decided that she had no choice but to take Lily and disappear. Anywhere.

She had done it before; she could do it again...

'Is that, No, you have it all wrong, Nick,' he probed softly, having seen that shake of her head. 'Or is it, I have no intention of confirming or denying that particular statement?'

Her eyes flashed deeply green as she glared across the table at him. 'Actually, I was thinking what a vivid imagination you have,' she returned tartly, leaning back as their used dishes were removed.

He shrugged. 'Running away won't work, Joey, don't you see that?' he sympathised gently.

That sympathy was almost her undoing. She had been struggling on alone for so long, it seemed, that for once she wanted to just break down and cry. But she wouldn't. Because if she started crying this time she just might not be able to stop!

She leant back in her chair, meeting Nick's gaze unblinkingly. 'Even supposing your theory was correct—which it isn't,' she added firmly, 'what makes you so sure it wouldn't work?'

Nick sighed. 'David Banning,' he answered with certainty. 'Surely you realise he's a man on a mission, Joey?' he continued hardly.

She frowned. 'I know he's interested in Lily's welfare—'

'But is he?' Nick pondered consideringly. 'He doesn't come over to me as a man who has any particularly strong interest in children—his own or anyone else's.'

'David doesn't have any children,' Joey answered distractedly.

'Why doesn't he?'

'Why don't you?' she returned impatiently. 'You're only a few years younger than he is,' she reasoned more calmly as she realised she was allowing him to get to her again.

'I've never been married,' Nick dismissed. 'But I know Banning has,' he added pointedly.

'Maybe his wife didn't want children,' she said irritably. 'Maybe they weren't married long enough. Does it really matter?'

'I'm not sure,' Nick said slowly. 'But I do mean to find out,' he added grimly.

Joey's eyes widened. 'What do you mean?'

He frowned. 'There's more to David Banning than meets the eye—and I mean to find out what there is!'

'How?' she breathed huskily.

Nick shrugged. 'There are ways. And means.'

As in a private detective—David's own ways and means of finding Lily and herself...

'No, Nick,' Joey protested agitatedly. 'Please leave it alone,' she pleaded. 'You'll only make the situation worse if David finds out that you've been checking up on him.'

Nick looked at her directly. '*Can* the situation get any worse?'

Oh, yes. Much, much worse...

'I— There are things you don't know, Nick.' She couldn't quite meet his gaze now. 'Things I don't talk about. To anyone. And I—I would rather you didn't antagonise David by—'

'What "things"?' Nick probed tensely, his gaze narrowed on the paleness of her face.

Joey shook her head. 'I've just told you, I don't talk about them. But I really don't want you checking up on David.' She swallowed hard. 'Just leave things as they are for the moment. Please!' She looked at him emotionally.

'So that you have time to disappear?' He was shaking his head even as he spoke. 'I can't let you do that, Joey—'

'You can't stop me! If that was what I intended doing,' she instantly corrected, her cheeks fiery red now as she realised the trap she had fallen into. She had become too relaxed, too comfortable in her life, these last six years.

'Oh, but I can,' he assured her softly.

Joey bristled indignantly. 'Just how do you intend doing that? And why would you even want to?' she questioned.

It was bad enough feeling as if David Banning was watching her every move, without this man starting too!

Nick looked at her intently. 'I'm sure you already know the answer to that,' he murmured gruffly.

She became suddenly still, reluctantly meeting the compelling darkness of his gaze. And at once wishing she hadn't! Because what she could see in those warm brown depths made her want to just melt into his arms. Something she couldn't do!

It was one thing to recognise that she was falling in love with this man, but quite another to realise that he might—only might!—return the feeling. It was a complication she simply couldn't deal with at the moment. Lily had to come first.

'David has asked me to marry him!'

The self-defensive statement was out before she could stop herself, and she instantly stared across at Nick in disbelief of her own words. It was the first indication she had given, even to herself, that she was seriously considering David's proposal...

Could she marry David? Could she seriously consider marrying a man she didn't love and who didn't love her? Could she uproot Lily, and herself, and move to America as David's wife? It sounded all too awful...!

But the alternative, she knew, was even more unpalatable...

Her look of consternation turned to one of defiance as she met Nick's narrow-eyed gaze. It was a look that said she would do what she had to do in order to cause as little pain to Lily, and herself, as was possible.

Nick's mouth was a thin, angry line. 'Why would he do that?' he rasped.

She flushed angrily. 'I'm not that unattractive!'

'That isn't in question; I've already told you you're a beautiful woman,' Nick dismissed grimly. 'David Banning's motivation in making the proposal, however, is very much in question.' He frowned darkly.

Joey wished she hadn't said anything now, wished she had just left things as they were. But it was too late for that; Nick now looked as if he was 'a man on a mission'!

'Besides,' Nick added harshly, 'as far as Banning is concerned, you're already engaged to marry me!'

She forced herself to relax, her smile faintly mocking. 'Obviously David isn't too convinced about that,' she derided. 'We both know it was only a ploy. One that evidently didn't come off,' she added drily.

Nick looked no less grim at her mockery. 'Perhaps it's time I had a private word with Banning—on the inadvisability of trying to poach another man's fiancée!'

Joey shook her head. 'What would be the point?'

'It would make me feel a whole lot better!' he snapped.

Joey couldn't help it—she laughed. And then marvelled

that she was still able to do such a thing in the midst of what was turning out to be worse than a Greek tragedy.

She was seriously in danger of having someone attempt to take Lily away from her. She was engaged to Nick, but not really. She was falling in love with him—for all the good it would do her. And David Banning had asked her to marry him. Which would mean that she didn't have to fight to keep Lily after all...

She shook her head, sobering as quickly as she had given way to laughter, deciding it was bordering on that earlier hysteria, anyway. 'I don't think making you ''feel a whole lot better'' is what any of this is about, Nick,' she countered harshly. 'The future happiness of a six-year-old child is the most important factor in all of this mess.'

His eyes had narrowed speculatively. 'Even at the price of your own?'

'Always,' Joey replied unhesitatingly, her own gaze clear and unwavering.

Nick was very still as he sat across the table from her. 'And has it always been that way? What were you doing with your life when you met Daniel Banning?' he probed sharply.

Her head went back defensively. 'What diff—?'

'Just tell me, hmm, Joey?' he rasped.

'I already had a degree in history; I had started my Masters in modern history,' she bit out dismissively.

Nick's brows rose in obvious surprise. 'Rather different from running a hairdressing salon, isn't it?' he murmured consideringly.

He could have no idea how different. Or the shock it had been to her life when she suddenly had Lily to take care of. In the circumstances, she had had no choice but to put her Masters on hold while she took care of Lily.

'My mother is a great advocate of having a second string

to one's bow,' she drawled. 'I trained as a hairdresser to earn money to put myself through university.' She shrugged.

'That doesn't exactly answer my question, does it?' Nick said shrewdly.

Joey raised innocent brows. 'Exactly what was the question?'

'Damn it, this is getting us nowhere,' he realised impatiently.

'Then why don't you just leave the subject alone? All of it,' she added pointedly.

Nick seemed to be fighting a battle within himself, sighing heavily as he came to some sort of decision. 'I may consider doing that. On one condition,' he replied slowly.

Her cheeks flushed. 'I don't think you're in any position to make conditions—'

'But I do,' he assured her confidently.

Joey wished, not for the first time, that she had never met this man, never involved him in the complication David Banning had brought into her life! 'What's the condition?' she prompted resentfully.

'I'll agree not to talk to Banning—for now—on condition that you don't disappear—or do something really stupid, such as accept his proposal!—before I can do some checking of my own—'

'What sort of checking?' she prompted sharply, more concerned with that at the moment than she was with being called 'stupid'!

Nick shrugged. 'On Banning, of course,' he returned mildly, giving her a considering look. 'What did you think I meant?' he probed shrewdly.

Joey turned away. 'I have no idea,' she dismissed lightly, smiling at the waiter as he brought the main course of their meal. 'Do you think I might actually be able to sit here in

peace and eat this?' she prompted Nick drily when they
were alone again.

'Once you've given me your word you won't just disappear without trace one night,' he invited tautly.

Joey gave an abrupt inclination of her head in agreement,
even as she picked up her knife and fork and began to
abstractedly eat the chicken salad.

She had thought her running days were over. Had
thought her life here with Lily was secure and settled.
David Banning had changed all that.

Where was it all going to end...?

'Mummy...?' Lily spoke slowly from the back of the car
later that evening as the two of them drove back from
swimming club.

Joey smiled briefly at her daughter in the driving mirror.
'Yes, Lily?'

'We won't ever leave here, will we?' Lily's still babyish
face was screwed up into a frown.

Joey's hands tightened instinctively on the steering wheel
as she tensed. 'What makes you ask something like that,
darling?' she prompted as lightly as she felt able. In the
circumstances.

If either David or Nick had said anything to Lily that
could possibly upset her...!

Lily moved her tiny shoulders in a shrug. 'It was something Daisy said at school today.'

Daisy? Hilary's daughter Daisy? What on earth could
Daisy know about what was going on in their lives at the
moment? Friend and confidante though Hilary was, Joey
hadn't been able to discuss this tangled mess even with her.

'We should be home in a few minutes, Lily; can we talk
about this then?' Joey suggested gently. This was neither
the time nor the place!

'Yes…' her daughter confirmed with obvious reluctance.

Joey was totally nonplussed at this strange twist in events, but she was very tired after a long day at work, and couldn't really give this subject her full attention while negotiating through Friday-evening traffic. Although that wasn't to say she wouldn't have liked to.

She had thought Lily, at least, was protected from the upheaval going on in the background of her life. But her worried question about leaving here seemed to imply otherwise. It was all Joey needed on the top of the disaster today was already proving to be. As every day was proving to be since David Banning's arrival in England!

'So what's worrying you, poppet?' she encouraged Lily once the two of them were comfortably ensconced on the sofa in their sitting-room at home, Lily snuggling within the warmth of Joey's arms.

Lily played awkwardly with a button on Joey's blouse. 'Daisy said something at break today,' she finally muttered.

'What did she say?' Joey prompted gently.

'That we were moving.' Lily's voice quivered emotionally.

Joey frowned. 'She did?' She knew that children often heard and saw things that adults weren't aware of, but at the same time she was absolutely certain she hadn't said anything to Hilary about this situation in front of Daisy.

In fact, a part of her kept hoping that the less she spoke of it to anyone, the higher the chance it would just go away!

'Head in the sand' came to mind, she acknowledged self-derisively, but she was quickly running out of options. And, despite her earlier compromise with Nick, it was this conversation with Lily that was in danger of robbing her of another one!

'Mmm.' Her daughter nodded, chewing on her bottom

lip. 'She says her mummy is worried because you're closing down the salon, and—'

'The salon!' Joey realised with relief, wondering if she might not be being given a reprieve, after all. It was about time something went her way! 'I'm only closing it down for a little while, darling,' she instantly reassured her. 'Just while I move to another location. I did explain to you a few weeks ago that someone has bought the land the salon is built on, and so I have to find somewhere else to go.'

Lily looked up worriedly into Joey's face. 'But does that mean we're moving from this house too? That I'll have to go to another school—?'

'Of course it doesn't,' she denied—realising even as she did so that she was probably boxing herself into a corner.

After her own precarious childhood, with her father often drinking away the money that should have been used to support his family, Joey had made a point of never letting Lily down, of always doing exactly what she said she would. But this time it could have serious repercussions.

'I did think the two of us might have a little holiday, though, while we're waiting to move into a new salon,' she continued lightly. 'Would you like that?'

'Yes…' Lily agreed uncertainly, her arms suddenly tightening around Joey's neck, obviously totally uninterested in the offer of a holiday. Even though she had so rarely had one. A brief visit to her grandmother in Ireland for Christmas two years ago was the sum total of what Joey had been able to afford in the way of holidays so far. 'I don't want to leave here, Mummy,' she added emotionally.

This had all been so much easier when Lily was a baby and barely aware of her surroundings, happy as long as Joey was never too far away from her. But the last two years, spent at school, making her own friends, had estab-

lished a life for Lily outside of the home they shared together. A life Lily obviously loved and didn't want to lose.

Joey hugged her daughter tightly. 'We aren't going to
leave here, Lily,' she assured her huskily. 'After all, this is
our home,' she added more fiercely.

Lily beamed up at her. 'I told Daisy she was wrong,' she
said knowingly. 'That you would have told me if we were
moving house too.'

Joey felt as if she had a huge lump wedged in her chest
later that evening as she stood in her daughter's bedroom
looking down at her innocently sleeping form, a slight
smile curving those still babyish lips.

Lily had such absolute faith in her, believed Joey had
the capacity to make everything right in her young world.
And until a few days ago Joey would have agreed with her.

Now she wasn't so sure…

CHAPTER TWELVE

'I WAS merely wondering if you had given my proposal any further thought?' David spoke mildly the following evening as he sat across from Joey in her sitting-room. Lily was already upstairs in bed when he had arrived a few minutes ago.

If she had given his proposal any more thought…!

Joey had thought of nothing else the last forty-eight hours, it seemed. A fact, she was sure, David Banning was all too well aware of.

How could she not have thought about it? If she married this man then all of her problems would be over, there would be no legal battle over Lily, and Lily would automatically take her place amongst the Banning family. It would all have been so neat and tidy. If only it had happened two months…two weeks ago…!

'I've thought about it,' she told David guardedly, her gaze narrowing slightly as she saw the instant blaze of triumph in his eyes. 'I'm still thinking about it,' she added hardly. 'After all, it's a life-changing decision, isn't it?' She shrugged.

'I suppose it is.' He adopted a pose of only casual interest. 'Although, as far as you and Lily are concerned, all on the plus side, I would have thought.' He looked pointedly down his arrogant nose at their clean but obviously compact surroundings.

Joey bristled resentfully, any of the softer feelings she might have started to feel towards this man two days ago instantly wiped out at this condescending attitude.

This house might not be up to the Banning standard, but she had worked hard for the initial down payment, and continued to do so in order to pay her mortgage each month. Obviously there would be no such worries if she was married to this man, but there were other circumstances to be taken into account.

'Aren't you forgetting something?' she returned sharply. 'My fiancé!' she reminded him at his questioning look.

He raised blond brows. 'I don't believe I'm the one forgetting that fact.'

She frowned. 'What do you mean?'

David shrugged. 'If you'll excuse my saying so, he doesn't seem to feature very largely in your life—'

'No, I won't "excuse you for saying so"!' Joey stood up agitatedly. 'Nick is a very busy man. As I'm sure, being a businessman yourself, you can appreciate only too well,' she added challengingly.

After a hard week at work, and an even harder time on a personal level, she had been looking forward to a Saturday evening of peace and calm; David's unexpected arrival a few minutes ago had certainly put an end to that!

'Of course,' David drawled. 'But never too busy to make time to spend with his beautiful fiancée, I would have thought. After all, it is the weekend.'

'So?' Joey tilted her chin.

'So why isn't he here?' David prompted.

'He has a business commitment in London,' she informed David triumphantly; Nick had telephoned her at the salon this morning to explain that he had an urgent appointment in town today, but that he would be back tomorrow.

David's mouth twisted humourlessly. 'Does he?'

Joey became suddenly still, not liking David's quiet confidence one little bit. 'I believe so,' she said guardedly.

David gave a scornful snort. 'Then you believe wrong, I'm afraid,' he drawled. 'At this precise moment—' he glanced casually at the gold watch on his wrist '—your fiancé is having dinner, in a rather elegant London restaurant, with a beautiful woman by the name of Barbara Dillon!' He announced the last triumphantly.

Joey felt the colour drain from her cheeks, her lips suddenly feeling numb. She had asked Nick at the beginning if there were any 'complications' to their bogus engagement, something he had been quick to assure her there weren't. Obviously, as she had half suspected at the time, he hadn't been completely truthful...

Not that it was really any of her business...

And what about those kisses the two of them had shared? came that traitorous voice inside her. What of the closeness that had been developing between them? The absolute trust, at being a man of his word, that she had given him? What did his date this evening with another woman—a beautiful woman!—make of all that?

'How can you possibly know all this?' she attacked angrily, her hands clenched into fists at her sides.

David raised blond brows. 'Guess!'

Joey's eyes widened as she suddenly realised exactly how David knew of Nick's movements this weekend. And possibly before that too...?

'You've had Nick followed,' she realised hollowly.

He gave a confirming inclination of his head. 'Only in my niece's interests, of course,' he drawled.

'Oh, of course!' Joey's eyes flashed angrily. 'How dare you?' she snapped furiously. 'Just who do you think you are? I—'

'The man is—was,' David corrected pointedly, 'destined to be my niece's stepfather! I have a perfect right to know what sort of man he is.' His mouth twisted with distaste.

'You may be able to condone his infidelity—perhaps that's the sort of relationship the two of you have?—but it's Lily's welfare that I—'

'My relationship with Nick is none of your business,' Joey cut in heatedly. 'And Lily's "welfare" has been my one concern for the last six years—'

'Has it?' David put in mildly.

'How dare you?' Joey repeated furiously, breathing deeply, two bright wings of colour in her cheeks now. 'You come over here, with only the scantest knowledge of Lily— or the life we've shared!—throwing out accusations and threats. And when they both fail to get you what you want you offer me marriage instead!' She shook her head disgustedly. 'I was considering your proposal—Mr Banning,' she rasped scathingly, 'but I don't need to consider it any longer. I wouldn't marry you now if you were the last man on earth!'

He appeared completely unruffled by her outburst, a humourless smile curving those mocking lips. 'An old—and well-worn—cliché,' he drawled derisively.

How dared he sit there mocking her? How dared he come here…?

It wasn't David Banning she was angry with, that traitorous little voice said softly inside her head. It was Nick she was furious with, Nick she wanted to scream and shout at. Because, despite all her best intentions, all her resolutions to the contrary, she *had* fallen in love with him. And this evening he was having dinner with another woman…

She turned sharply away. 'Would you just leave?' she asked David Banning in a flatly unemotional voice.

Because a part of her was numb. With the knowledge that she had committed the biggest folly of her life. How could she have fallen in love with Nick Mason…?

'Why don't you just bow to the inevitable, Joey?' Instead

of leaving, David had moved to stand only inches behind her, the warmth of his breath stirring the tendrils of hair at her nape. 'It really wouldn't be so bad being married to me,' he continued lightly. 'Your future, and Lily's, would be secure. And as for our own relationship...I have my own life to lead. And I would leave you to live yours. Within reason,' he added hardly. 'And with discretion, obviously.'

It sounded exactly the sort of marriage Joey most despised. At least most couples seemed to start off their married life together in love with each other. Relationships only deteriorated to the compromise David was suggesting with the passing of years. To start off a marriage with so little expectation of its success made her feel nauseous.

She shook her head without turning. 'I couldn't live like that,' she told him. 'At worst, it's calculated. At the least, it's dishonest.'

'It makes sense,' he snapped harshly.

'No.' Joey gave another shake of her head as she turned to face David, her head high as she found herself in such close proximity with him they were almost touching. 'I— I'm sure your offer is a good one, David, but...I really can't marry you.'

Which left her with only one alternative...

And why not? She only had to keep the salon open one more week, Lily had only one more week at school until the summer holidays began, and she was halfway packed already.

But what of the promise she had made Nick...?

In view of how he was spending his evening, that promise now seemed slightly ridiculous!

'Why the hell not?' David rasped, obviously displeased by her answer.

She drew in a ragged breath. 'I just can't.' She shook her head.

'Because of Mason?' he derided hardly, blue eyes glittering scathingly. 'I've already told you how he's spending his weekend!' he scorned.

Yes, he had—and it made not the slightest difference to how Joey felt about him!

She was the one who kept reminding Nick that they only had a business arrangement, a bargain. She had also told him of David's proposal, and that she was thinking about it. In those circumstances, what had she expected Nick to do?

Not go off to London to spend the evening—and night?—with another woman!

'No, not just because of Nick,' she answered David cautiously.

'Then what is it?' David reached out and clasped her arms. 'You would want a real marriage, is that it?' he rasped, gaze narrowed searchingly on the paleness of her face.

With this man? No. Most definitely no!

With Nick?

Oh, yes...!

How had this happened to her? Why had it? And why now?

She was thirty years old, well past the age to be fooled by romantic illusions—any of those she might or might not have had had been wiped out by Daniel seven years ago, anyway! And yet she had fallen in love with Nick, a man who had been kind to her, yes, and who had quickly built up a rapport with Lily, too. But how could she have allowed herself to fall in love with him...?

'No, I don't want that, either,' she answered dully.

'Then what do you want?' David thrust her away from him, glaring at her frustratedly.

She wanted what every other woman and man, in varying

degrees, wanted—someone in her life that she loved, and who loved her in return. Was that expecting too much? Going on her life to date, it would appear so...

She gave a sad smile. 'Why can't we just leave things as they are?'

'Because...' He broke off, drawing in a deep, controlling breath.

Joey looked at him frowningly. 'Because...?'

'Because it isn't practical,' David clipped out abruptly. 'If things stay as they are you would want to continue to live in England with Lily—'

'Of course,' she confirmed.

'Exactly.' He nodded in acknowledgement. 'Joey, my parents are no longer young. They rarely travel, and certainly don't leave the States any more. Which means that Lily would have to travel to America to visit them—something you have already told me you aren't happy about—'

'I'm not.' Joey shook her head emphatically.

It would be so unfair to Lily to subject her to that upheaval every few months or so. She was only six, for goodness' sake!

'As I've already said, the arrangement, as it stands, is completely impractical.' David shrugged implacably.

Joey knew that, had already gone round and round in her own head with these same thoughts. Only to find, as David had, that there was no cut-and-dried answer. All she had succeeded in doing was giving herself a headache.

'Why, oh, why did Daniel have to die?' she choked emotionally, the beginnings of that headache starting to pound inside her head once again.

David's expression instantly softened. 'So you did care for him after all,' he said slowly. 'I had begun to wonder,' he murmured at her sharp look.

It had been too long since she had last seen Daniel to

know what she'd felt towards him any more. What she did
know was that if he hadn't died when he had none of this
would be happening to her! And to her beloved Lily...

The passing of the years had softened the anger she felt
towards Daniel for what had happened almost seven years
ago, had numbed the edges of her pain. But David
Banning's arrival here had brought that all back into sharp
focus.

'"Care for him"?' she repeated scathingly as she looked
up at David with angry green eyes. 'He was, without a
doubt, the most selfish person I have ever known,' she bit
out coldly.

Even in death, Daniel continued to hurt. To destroy. As
he had in life.

She had lived in dread, the first year of Lily's life, of
Daniel changing his mind and coming back to claim Lily
as his daughter, had quaked with fear almost every time
the telephone or doorbell rang. But it had never happened.
Not once, in almost seven years, had Daniel even attempted
to see his daughter, let alone wanted to acknowledge Lily
as being his.

Instead his older brother, David, had come to make that
claim after Daniel's death.

David had stiffened at her angry words, his expression
hardening, his eyes narrowed to steely slits. 'Perhaps,' he
conceded tautly. 'But that really changes nothing, does it?'
he scorned. 'I intend remaining at the hotel until Monday
morning, Joey. I would appreciate it if you could give me
an answer before then.'

'But I—'

'Sleep on it, Joey,' David advised drily as she would
have reminded him she had already given him that answer.
'And while you're doing so,' he added softly as he moved

towards the door, 'give some thought to where Nick Mason is sleeping tonight!' He quietly let himself out of the house.

His parting shot was designed to wound—and it succeeded!

Joey sat down as her knees gave way, burying her face in her hands as the tears began to fall.

Only six days ago—six days!—she had been a woman in control of her own life, had had all of her systems worked out so that she could be a good mother to Lily as well as work to support them both. How could she possibly have guessed a week ago the chaos her life was to become? What was happening over Lily's future was awful enough, but...

How could Joey possibly have guessed a week ago that she would fall in love with Nick Mason?

Or that Nick was spending tonight with another woman...?

'Aren't you going to invite me in?' Nick teased lightly as Joey silently faced him as he stood on her doorstep the following afternoon, having opened the door to his ring only seconds ago.

He looked—marvellous, Joey acknowledged miserably as she continued to look at him: that handsome face glowing with good humour, lithe and attractive in a cream T-shirt and faded denims.

Obviously a night in bed with the 'beautiful' Barbara Dillon suited him!

'What do you want, Nick?' she prompted, making no effort to 'invite him in.

His smile faded as he began to frown. 'I've only been away just over twenty-four hours, Joey; what the hell happened in that time?'

It was twenty-four hours he had spent in the arms of another woman!

Oh, Joey knew their bogus engagement gave her no right to object to anything Nick did—that he was a free agent, could spend his time how he pleased. But that didn't mean she had to like it!

'Nothing,' she sighed. 'Absolutely nothing,' she added dully.

Nick looked unconvinced. 'You don't look as if it were nothing,' he said slowly, his gaze narrowed on her deliberately expressionless face. 'Has Banning—?'

'Have you had a nice weekend, Nick?' Joey cut in firmly.

'Not bad,' he replied offhandedly. 'Although it isn't over yet,' he added pointedly.

Joey's cheeks flushed with resentment at his implication that his weekend enjoyment had taken a definite nosedive in the last few minutes. 'I'm rather busy today, Nick, so if that's all you came here to say—'

'It isn't,' he cut in sharply, pushing the door completely open before striding into the house.

Joey slowly followed him through to the sitting-room, her head back challengingly as his sharp gaze took in the packing boxes that littered the room, before turning back to her, dark brows raised questioningly.

'I thought we had an agreement,' he rasped harshly.

'We did,' she acknowledged flatly.

That agreement had ended the moment she knew Nick was spending the weekend with another woman. She had accepted then that she was the only one really looking out for Lily's welfare. Nick had left her on Friday with the idea that he was still intent on helping her, but his behaviour since certainly didn't give that impression! As such, Joey had decided to deal with the situation in the only way she knew how.

'Did?' Nick repeated softly.

Joey turned away. 'David is going back to America in the morning—'

'And you're going with him!' Nick finished hardly.

She gave a humourless laugh. 'No,' she dismissed.

'Then you're running away, after all,' Nick said grimly.

'I prefer to think of it as—relocating,' she corrected carefully, realising as she did so that that was exactly what she had told Lily they wouldn't do.

But what choice did she have?

Lily, she hoped, would forgive her. In time.

'Same difference,' Nick dismissed scathingly.

Her eyes flashed angrily. 'You—'

'Where's Lily today?' He looked around them, the silence in the house telling him it was empty apart from themselves.

'Why?' she challenged.

He shrugged. 'Just curious.'

'She's at a birthday party until five o'clock,' Joey supplied defensively.

'So you thought you would take the opportunity of her absence to pack,' Nick guessed grimly. 'Joey, have you any idea what you're contemplating doing to that child—?'

'Don't come here and start lecturing me on how best to take care of my own daughter!' Joey snapped furiously, her body tense, looking very slender in fitted green T-shirt and faded denims. But her defences slowly crumbled as Nick merely continued to look at her with compassionate eyes. 'I just don't know what else to do!' she finally groaned emotionally, burying her face in her hands.

He sighed, stepping forward to take her into his arms. 'You could start by trusting me.' He spoke huskily into the softness of her hair as it cascaded over her shoulders.

Trusting him…! He had spent most of the previous

day—and probably the night, too!—in the company of another woman; how could she possibly trust him?

She shook her head. 'This doesn't have the same...priority for you as it does for me,' she choked. 'I'm in danger of losing my daughter, and all you can do is—' She broke off abruptly as she realised what she had been about to say.

It was one thing to feel like a jealous fiancée, something else completely to actually start to sound like one! They had a bargain, nothing more. And she must never forget that!

'"All I can do..."?' Nick prompted tensely.

She pulled back, shaking her head as she did so. 'Never mind,' she dismissed, desperately fighting to regain control of her emotions.

If only Nick didn't look so strong and dependable, so attractive, so... God, how she wanted this man!

Some of her emotions must have shown in her face, and Nick's eyes darkened until they looked almost black, his gaze sensual as it locked on the softness of her mouth.

'Joey...!'

'No!' She pulled out of his arms as he would have kissed her, putting as much distance between them as she could in the close confines of the sitting-room. 'That only... complicates things even more, Nick,' she told him hardly, her nails digging into the palms of her hands as she resisted the impulse to move back into his arms. 'I'm very grateful for the help you've tried to give me—'

'But?'

'But it hasn't worked.' She sighed. 'David is still intent on uprooting Lily and taking her to America—'

'He's told you that?' Nick's eyes were narrowed speculatively.

'Yes.' There was no point in prevarication.

'What happened to his marriage proposal?' Nick persisted.

She grimaced. 'I turned him down.'

Nick gave a deep sigh of relief. 'That's something, at least. But if he's going back to America in the morning—'

'He's coming back, Nick,' she said with certainty. 'And, unless I'm mistaken, next time he'll be armed with more than just a marriage proposal!'

Nick shook his head. 'A court order would stop him—'

'No!' Joey cut in sharply, unable to stop the fear from rising within her. A fear she must not let Nick see! 'No, Nick,' she repeated in a much calmer voice. 'I don't want to drag Lily through the courts.'

He looked puzzled. 'Why not?'

'I just don't, OK?' Her eyes flashed warningly.

'No, it's not OK. What are you so afraid of—?'

'I'm not afraid,' Joey cut in fiercely. 'I just—I don't want Lily's childhood ruined by a legal wrangle.' A legal wrangle she knew she had no certainty of winning...

Nick stared at her uncomprehendingly. 'And what happens when Banning finds you?'

'I'll move on again,' she assured him firmly.

'And again? And again? However many times it takes?' he guessed grimly. 'Joey, you can't do that to Lily.' He shook his head. 'Far better to get this sorted out legally now—'

'And what would you know about it?' she challenged tautly.

How could he imagine, even guess, the pain of possibly losing your daughter? He couldn't. But it was a possibility Joey had lived with every day of the last six and a half years...

A possibility she would continue to live with while there

was even a chance that the Banning family could claim Lily for their own!

'I think you had better go, Nick,' she said dully. 'I have to finish my packing.'

He stared at her frustratedly, obviously not understanding her vehemence.

And he never would.

The fewer people who knew the reason for that, the better.

'Joey, the real reason I came here this afternoon was to tell you I'm flying to New York later this evening.' Nick spoke slowly, pointedly.

Her gaze sharpened. 'Why?'

As if she really needed to ask! It seemed she was wrong, that he hadn't given up on helping her, after all—amazing, considering he had spent most of yesterday with another woman! But in the circumstances, to stir up more interest in Lily with the Banning family could only make matters worse.

Nick shrugged. 'I've found out Banning has been—economical with the facts, shall we say?' he said carefully.

How on earth had he managed to do that in the midst of spending time with the beautiful Barbara Dillon?

She frowned. 'In what way?'

Nick shook his head. 'That's what I need to go to New York to find out.'

Joey's frown deepened, totally bewildered now. 'You would do that for me?'

His expression softened as he looked at her. 'Not too many people have been kind to you in the past, have they, Joey?' he guessed huskily.

She didn't answer. It wasn't a statement that needed an answer; the facts spoke for themselves. Besides, she was too emotionally choked at the moment to be able to speak, knew that she would break down completely if she even tried.

She had got through the last six and a half years by not allowing, or expecting, any help from other people. Even the help she and Hilary gave each other was kept on a business level; Hilary was her employee rather than anything else. Because, as Joey knew only too well, the less you expected of other people, the less you would be disappointed when they ultimately let you down.

But Nick's offer to go to New York was outside the limits of their business arrangement...

'Yes, I would do that for you, Joey,' Nick answered briskly, seeming to sense the weakness in her defences—and knowing she hated it. 'All I want from you is a promise—a definite promise,' he added firmly, 'that you will stay put until I get back. Will you do that for me?' He looked at her intently.

'That really depends on how long you intend being away.' Her mouth twisted humourlessly. 'Will you be back by the end of the week?' she frowned.

'I had better be,' he chuckled. 'Otherwise my father might just decide to sack me!'

Joey doubted that very much, had already gathered that Nick's was a close family. Besides, despite what Nick said about it being his father's company, Joey could see that Nick did most of the physical toing and froing involved.

'All right,' she agreed. 'But I want you to know I'm going to carry on packing, anyway,' she warned him.

If Nick failed to find out anything that was going to help her keep Lily then she would have to move quickly after his return. There was no point in letting him think anything else.

'You do that,' he encouraged enigmatically, moving to

grasp her lightly by the shoulders before bending and kissing her lightly on the lips. 'I'll be back soon,' he promised.

She swallowed hard, desperately fighting the impulse to throw herself into his arms and plead with him to make everything right for her.

Because she knew, ultimately, that he couldn't do that?

Or was it because she knew, once in Nick's arms, she wouldn't want to leave them?

'Call me,' she encouraged huskily instead, knowing that it would be sheer torture to just sit here waiting, with no word from Nick at all.

He nodded grimly. 'As soon as I know anything,' he promised.

Joey didn't move for a long time after Nick had left to go to the hotel and collect his things ready for his trip to New York.

Exactly what had he already found out about David?

And could it really make any difference to the outcome of this mess?

Somehow, despite Nick's confidence, she doubted that. But, as she was also only too well aware, Nick was the only hope she had at the moment...

CHAPTER THIRTEEN

'But why can't you tell me now, Nick?' Joey demanded exasperatedly. 'The line isn't bugged, you know,' she added impatiently—forgetting completely, in her agitation, the skip her heartbeat had given a few minutes ago just at the sound of Nick's voice down the telephone line.

'I'm well aware of that, Joey,' Nick came back drily, his voice so clear it sounded as if he were in the next room rather than still thousands of miles away in New York. 'Look, I'm packing now; I will be with you tomorrow afternoon—'

'That isn't the point,' she interrupted irritably; the last two days of waiting to hear from Nick had been long enough, without this added tension. 'Why can't you just tell me now?'

If it was good news, surely Nick would want to put her mind at rest immediately, rather than make her wait until he returned tomorrow afternoon?

But Nick was far from stupid—probably knew that if he was to tell her bad news over the telephone there was every possibility she would run before he even got back to England...

'It's nothing bad, Joey.' Nick seemed to immediately pick up on her troubled thoughts. 'In fact... The salon is closed tomorrow afternoon, isn't it?'

'Yes,' she confirmed slowly, surprised, with the busy life Nick seemed to lead, that he had remembered Wednesday was half-day closing at the salon.

'Keep it free,' he told her firmly.

'Nick—'

'Joey, for once could you just do what I ask without arguing, hmm?' he cut in. 'Nothing bad is going to happen,' he assured her in a gentler voice as he seemed to realise he was being a bit harsh with her. 'In fact, everything I've found out is positive rather than negative.'

'And that's as much as you're going to tell me,' Joey guessed drily.

'Yes,' Nick confirmed, laughter in his voice.

'I… Have you seen David while you've been there?' She presumed the other man had kept to his plan of returning to America on Monday morning. She certainly hadn't contacted him, hoping her silence had given him her answer to his proposal!

'I've seen him,' Nick answered grimly.

Joey tensed. 'And?'

'Tomorrow, Joey,' Nick promised lightly.

'But—'

'I bet you were the sort of little girl who went around the house weeks before Christmas, looking in all the cupboards and drawers for your presents rather than waiting for the surprise on Christmas morning,' he teased.

Then he would have bet wrong; there had been few presents in her family home, at Christmas or any other time. Her mother had done her best to make it a festive occasion, but with a husband who drank away money rather than providing presents for his wife and children it had usually quickly deteriorated into just yet another day of arguments and tension.

'Maybe,' Joey murmured noncommittally. 'Do you want me to meet you at the airport?' Even the thought of driving through the heavy airport traffic would be better than sitting at home waiting for Nick to arrive!

'It's been a long time since anyone met me at the airport…!' He sounded surprised at the offer. 'But, no, thanks, Joey; I drove myself to the airport and left my car parked there for my return,' he drawled ruefully.

'Oh, OK,' Joey muttered frustratedly. 'I'll just have to wait here, then, won't I?'

'Yes, you will.' Again the smile could be heard in Nick's voice at her obviously disgruntled tone. 'How's the packing going?' he added lightly.

'Slowly, with Lily around and work to do,' she admitted wryly.

'That reminds me… I've spoken to my father about letting you have one of the units at the supermarket—'

'I told you not to do that!' she gasped.

When had he done that? It was Tuesday evening now—the first time Nick had telephoned her since he had left her on Sunday afternoon. But he hadn't been too busy to talk to his father, it seemed…!

'Neither of us seem to respond too well to being "told" what to do, do we?' he returned ruefully. 'Something we'll have to work on when I get back,' he added huskily.

Joey's fingers tightened around the telephone receiver. Exactly what did he mean by that remark?

'Anyway, to get back to my original subject…' Nick drawled derisively.

What had been his original subject? Joey couldn't remember. Just talking to Nick on the telephone seemed to throw her into a state of confusion. Just the sound of his voice made her tremble with longing…!

'My father is in complete agreement with letting you have one of the units at a reasonable rent,' Nick continued briskly. 'If you're still interested, of course,' he added enigmatically. 'But we'll talk about that further when I get home, too!'

Home… Did he mean London? Or did he mean something else?

Whoa, Joey, she instantly instructed herself, don't let your imagination run away with you. Just because she ached to see Nick again, it did not mean he felt the same way about her. In fact, with the beautiful Barbara Dillon in his life, she was sure he didn't!

Although there was no getting away from the fact that Nick had gone to New York for the sole purpose of helping her. At least, she assumed that he had. The fact that he had been in contact with his father while he was there seemed to imply that perhaps she had been wrong about that too…

'Yes,' she confirmed dully. 'I'll see you tomorrow afternoon, then.'

'You most certainly will,' he said with certainty. 'And please don't worry, Joey; everything will work out. You'll see,' he assured her before ringing off.

Don't worry, Nick had said. Easier said than done! She had done nothing but worry since the moment David Banning had appeared outside her house just over a week ago.

And she continued to worry as she waited at home on Wednesday afternoon for Nick to arrive. When he hadn't done so by three-fifteen, Joey knew she had no choice but to go out and collect Lily and Daisy from school. She hoped he wouldn't arrive while she was out as she spent more precious moments dropping Daisy off at her home, before returning with Lily.

The street where they lived was completely empty of cars as Joey parked outside her house—most people were still out at work. There was certainly no battered pick-up in sight!

Where was Nick? Joey fretted as she got some juice and

biscuits for Lily. He had said he would be back this afternoon, and it was almost four-thirty now. She—

The doorbell. At last!

Her heart did more than skip a beat when she opened the door and saw Nick standing outside—it seemed to stop altogether! And as for breathing—she seemed to have forgotten how!

'Joey,' he greeted her huskily, eyes that warm chocolate brown as he looked at her.

He looked wonderful, she acknowledged achingly: dark hair slightly windswept, that handsome face creased into a boyish smile, his body lithely muscular beneath a dark brown leather jacket worn over a white shirt and blue denims.

But no doubt, she reminded herself firmly, the beautiful Barbara Dillon found him just as irresistible!

'Where have you been?' Joey asked accusingly. 'I expected you hours ago!' she fell back on anger as her defence against the urge she had to just launch herself into his arms.

His smile faded slightly, a frown forming between his eyes. 'There were a few…delays in New York. It meant I had to get a later flight than I intended.' He shrugged. 'But I'm here now.'

There was no doubting that fact; the erratic beating of her heart and the tightness in her chest were testament to that!

'Obviously,' she noted scathingly. 'Then I suppose you had better…' She broke off, her attention caught—and held—by a movement behind Nick.

A black BMW was parked behind Joey's own car—obviously Nick didn't always drive around in a battered pickup!—and two people were slowly emerging from inside it.

Two people Joey instantly recognised!

The man getting out of the front passenger seat of the car was an older—much older—version of Daniel and David Banning. His hair was white, rather than blond, but he stood as tall and handsome as the two younger men.

Joey's gaze moved frantically to the woman getting out of the back of the car. A woman who, although obviously aged in her late sixties or early seventies, nevertheless looked exactly like Lily!

Joey knew, without the shadow of a doubt, that these two people were Daniel's parents. Lily's grandparents! And Nick—*Nick*—had brought them here!

How could he?

What had he done…?

Joey swayed slightly, all the colour having drained from her face. Her first instinct was to run back into the house and lock the door. But at the same time she knew that would achieve nothing. Besides, at the moment she felt too weak to run anywhere…!

'Steady.' Nick reached out to grasp her arm, frowning his concern. 'Joey—'

'How could you?' Joey breathed in a broken whisper as her knees seemed in danger of collapsing beneath her. 'Oh, Nick, how could you do this to me?'

His hand tightened on her arm. 'It was the only way, Joey,' he told her firmly. 'They don't mean you any harm,' he assured her as Joey continued to look at him, her eyes swimming with tears. 'They just—'

'You don't understand,' Joey choked, shaking her head distractedly as she wrenched herself free of his hand. 'You just don't understand what you've done!' she cried again as the elderly couple walked slowly towards them, Joey staring at them like a victim caught in a viper's gaze.

This couldn't be happening!

It was her worst nightmare come true.

Someone had to tell her it wasn't happening!

Please...!

'Joey?' The elderly woman spoke gently as the couple finally reached them, her smile warm, if a little uncertain.

The smile that was so like Lily's...!

She closed her eyes briefly, willing this scene to have disappeared when she opened them again.

It hadn't!

'I'll never forgive you for this, Nick,' Joey told him vehemently as she turned to look at him accusingly. 'Never!' she repeated fiercely.

Nick had gone pale beneath his tan, a nerve pulsing at his jaw. 'They haven't come here to hurt you, Joey.'

'You have no idea!' She shook her head distractedly.

'Joey.' The elderly man spoke softly. 'I hope you'll allow me to call you Joey...?' he prompted gently.

She swallowed the nausea that was threatening to engulf her. 'Whatever.' She shrugged resignedly, her voice huskily low. She felt as if the weight of the world had suddenly dropped down onto her shoulders. And knew she didn't feel strong enough to carry it.

The elderly man nodded, smiling slightly. 'Nick is quite right when he tells you we haven't come here to hurt you,' he told her. 'Perhaps we should introduce ourselves first, hmm? I'm Samuel Banning and this is my wife—Lilian.'

Joey stared at the elderly woman as the last of the colour drained from her cheeks. Lilian. How...?

She shook her head dazedly. Not only did Lily look like her grandmother, she had been named after her too.

'Could we all go inside, do you think, Joey?' Nick prompted as the first of the cars started arriving back outside the houses in the road as people returned home from work.

Inside? Lily was inside. Was even now sitting innocently

in the kitchen drinking her juice and eating her biscuits. With no idea of the change that was about to take place in her young life!

Lilian Banning reached out and briefly grasped Joey's arm reassuringly. 'Perhaps that would be best, dear,' she encouraged gently.

Best for who?

Certainly not for her and Lily.

But it was too late for that. Too late for anything but the truth now. A truth that threatened to destroy her, and everything she held dear in life.

'Yes,' she accepted heavily, standing to one side to allow the elderly couple to precede her into the empty sitting-room. Lily was obviously still in the kitchen.

'We'll join you in a moment,' Nick told the other couple grimly, holding tightly onto Joey's arm as he pulled the door slightly closed behind them. 'What is it?' he asked frowningly. 'What is it you aren't telling me, Joey?' he prompted shrewdly.

'Nothing,' she answered dully, looking up at him with pained eyes. 'No wonder you wouldn't tell me what was going on when we spoke on the telephone last night.' She grimaced. 'You knew I wouldn't still be here if you told me you were bringing the Bannings back with you.'

'Originally it was only going to be Samuel; Lilian hasn't been well and really shouldn't travel. But she was determined to see her granddaughter. It was that determination that meant we had to rearrange the travel arrangements and take a later flight,' he explained.

Joey shook her head. 'If you're trying to make me feel bad because so far I've been less than welcoming then you're out of luck!' she told him with a return of her anger. 'The situation you have helped to create here is...' She gave a shaky sigh. 'It's catastrophic!'

'Then tell me,' he encouraged frustratedly. 'Maybe I can help—'

'I think you've already "helped" enough,' she told him disgustedly, before turning and entering the sitting-room, uncaring of whether Nick joined them or not; his presence now was completely superfluous. 'I'm sorry about that...' She broke off her apology, her face paling once again as she saw Lily enter the room from the kitchen, having finished her juice and biscuits.

The likeness between Lily and her paternal grandmother was all the more obvious, seeing the two of them together like this!

Although probably not to Lily, Joey acknowledged as her daughter gave her a quizzical look at finding yet two more strangers in her home in as many weeks.

Joey watched the Bannings, her breath catching painfully in her chest as she saw the tears in Lilian Banning's eyes as she looked at her granddaughter for the first time; Samuel Banning was having to swallow emotionally too.

'Come and say hello, darling,' Joey invited huskily, holding out her hand encouragingly to Lily even as she sensed Nick entering the room behind her. 'This is Samuel and Lilian Banning.' She held Lily's hand as she made the introductions. 'Uncle David's mummy and daddy,' she added, knowing that, at almost seven, her daughter was quite capable of adding two and two together and coming up with the appropriate answer.

Lily frowned in concentration. 'Does that make them my—?'

'Grandparents,' Joey finished lightly. 'Yes, this is your granny and grandad from America,' she confirmed. 'They've come all this way just to see you,' she added fairly.

Lily's eyes opened wide with amazement as she turned

back to the elderly couple, obviously trying to take in their relationship to her. 'Hello,' she finally managed to say shyly.

'Hello, Lily.' Lilian Banning was the first one to speak. 'You—you look very like your father,' she managed to choke, before tears began to fall down her lined cheeks.

Samuel Banning took a protective step forward. 'Lilian—'

'Don't cry, Granny.' Lily was the one to comfort her, moving to stand beside the elderly lady, putting her arm about the shaking shoulders. 'Please don't cry,' she pleaded as she laid her head against her grandmother's shoulder.

Which only made the elderly lady cry all the more as she gathered Lily tightly into her arms.

Joey was crying too as she watched them, could feel the heat of the tears against her cheeks.

She was crying for Lilian. For Lily. But most of all for herself. Because she knew beyond the shadow of a doubt that she had just lost her daughter...

CHAPTER FOURTEEN

'LILY is absolutely adorable, Joey,' Lilian Banning told her softly, the five of them having walked to a nearby park. Samuel Banning and Nick were taking it in turns to push Lily on a swing as the two women sat on a wooden bench watching them.

At least, Joey had thought they were both watching Lily...

She turned to see Lilian Banning looking at her with warm sympathy. Which was almost her undoing!

The situation had been far from easy when she had first been left alone with Lily. Her own parents had been sympathetic, but at the same time believed she should carry on with her Masters and give the baby up for adoption. Something Joey had vowed she could never do!

And so she had battled to keep Lily from the onset, never looking for help from anyone—and never being disappointed when there was none forthcoming! This woman's obvious understanding of her plight made Joey want to just sit and cry. Oh, to have someone else take charge for a change! Except the Bannings were the last people she could allow to do that!

'Yes,' she confirmed dully.

Lilian reached out and lightly squeezed her arm. 'Believe me, Joey, we're only here to help,' she assured softly. 'But we'll talk of this further once Lily is in bed, hmm?' she encouraged as a happily laughing Lily jumped from the swing and ran towards them.

Joey didn't answer, standing up in time to catch her

daughter as she threw herself into her arms, swinging her round and round, as she'd used to when Lily was a baby.

They were both laughing, flushed and slightly breathless, when they came to a halt—clinging to each other to maintain their balance, receiving indulgent glances from several people out taking an early-evening stroll in the park.

This must all look so normal to them, Joey realised sadly: the doting grandparents, the laughing mother, the indulgent—well, Nick couldn't exactly be called Lily's anything, but to an outsider it would no doubt appear that he was Lily's father.

All so normal—and at the same time so completely abnormal!

But, to the credit of all of them, Lily remained completely innocent of the undercurrents that surrounded this happy scene.

And she continued to do so while they all went and had a meal in a local pub, obviously relishing this unexpected treat, protesting loudly when Joey suggested it was time to leave. Nick's answer to that was to pick her up, throw her over his shoulder and carry the giggling Lily home that way.

'This evening was fun, wasn't it, Mummy?' Lily smiled up sleepily, but happily, at Joey later, once she had been tucked up in bed.

Fun?

Oh, the Bannings were nice people, were obviously already besotted with their young granddaughter. And Nick, in his chosen role of go-between, had neatly stepped in to fill any awkward moments that had arisen through the evening. Joey, for her part, had pointedly not spoken a word to him since they'd entered the house together earlier. He couldn't know what he had done by bringing the Bannings here, but Joey was still too upset with him to be able to talk to him politely.

So, no, Joey couldn't exactly say this evening had been fun. And she was very much aware it was going to get worse!

'Time for sleep now, young lady,' she told Lily firmly before bending to kiss her daughter goodnight. 'Granny and Granddad will still be here tomorrow.' She answered her daughter's next question before she could even ask it.

And the next day. And the next. And the next. As long as it took for them to take Lily from her...!

Well, it wasn't a complete *fait accompli*; she did have rights of her own. Rights of love and caring, if nothing else!

She drew in a deep controlling breath before entering the sitting-room, knowing that battle was probably about to commence. But it was a battle Nick had no part of...

'I think it might be better if you left now,' she told him stiffly, once back in the sitting-room.

'I disagree,' he drawled as he sat in one of the armchairs while the Bannings sat close together on the sofa, looking perfectly relaxed and her dismissive words doing nothing to change that.

Joey sighed frustratedly, knowing there were things about the following conversation that she did not want him to hear. They were too personal, too—painful.

She drew in a ragged breath. 'Nick—'

'I think he should stay, Joey.' Samuel Banning was the one to cut in gently.

Her head went back defensively. 'On the basis I'm going to need all the moral support I can get?' she said tautly.

The elderly man smiled sadly, shaking his head. 'On the basis that he's your fiancé. That he obviously cares for you and Lily very much.'

Well, Nick hadn't told the other couple that their engagement was a sham; that was something, at least! Although that still didn't change the fact that she would rather he wasn't present during this conversation.

'I'm staying, Joey,' Nick told her implacably, effectively putting an end to any further objections she might have tried to make.

Unless she made a complete scene about it. Which, in the circumstances, Joey was loath to do.

'Fine. Stay, then,' she allowed impatiently, before turning challengingly to the Bannings. 'I want you to know from the outset that I will not give Lily up without a fight!'

Samuel nodded. 'That's very much to your credit if—'

Her eyes flashed deeply green. 'Please don't patronise me—'

'If we intended fighting you for custody of her,' Samuel continued firmly. 'Which we don't,' he added softly.

'You...' Joey froze as his quietly spoken words penetrated her anger. 'You don't?' she echoed disbelievingly.

Samuel shook his head ruefully. 'Joey, I am seventy-eight and Lilian is seventy-five; what possible long-term use could we be to a little girl of six?'

Joey stared at him, hope beginning to well up inside her. A hope that she quickly quelled—it really couldn't be this easy. There had to be a catch attached to this somewhere.

'Joey, Samuel and I are well-aware of the personal sacrifices you have made in order to take care of Lily,' Lilian put in huskily.

Joey looked sharply at the older woman. She couldn't know. No one in this room knew the truth but her. Did they...?

'I was very familiar with Daniel's—faults, Joey,' Lilian continued ruefully. 'I know how irresponsible he was, how selfish at times. But, at the same time, he and I were very close,' she added huskily.

'Meaning?' Joey looked at the other woman with wary eyes.

'Meaning, my son was able to talk to me as he did to no one else.' Lilian shrugged. 'For instance, he told me he had fallen in love with a girl while at Oxford. That they had loved each other,' she added softly.

Joey sensed rather than saw Nick move uncomfortably in his chair. She had no idea why he should do so—only knew he should have left when she'd asked him to.

'And what about Lily? Did he tell you about her, too?' she challenged the older woman, unable to actually look at Nick. If she did, loving him as she did, she wouldn't be able to carry on with this conversation!

Lilian's lips trembled emotionally as she sought to keep control. 'Unfortunately, no,' she finally answered. 'If he had—'

'You would have come over here and tried to take her away from me all the sooner!' Joey guessed scathingly. 'I—'

'I meant it when I said we weren't here to do that, Joey.' Samuel Banning was the one to answer her soothingly. 'I'll make you a promise of that,' he assured her as she still looked unconvinced. 'And, although you may find it hard to believe, I am a man of my word.'

Joey frowned. 'Why should I find that hard to believe?' Although she did still find it hard to believe him when he said he had no intention of attempting to take Lily from her...!

His mouth firmed angrily. 'My youngest son left you literally ''holding the baby''. And I believe my eldest son has been making your life a little...uncomfortable—shall we say?—this last week,' he bit out tautly, blue eyes steely.

That had to be the understatement of the evening! David Banning had been making her life hell for the last week.

'Let me assure you that he won't be bothering you again,' Samuel continued grimly.

Joey looked at him frowningly. 'He won't...?'

'No,' the elderly man answered emphatically. 'David has—problems of his own that he needs to sort out. I have suggested he stays in the States—well away from you and Lily—and does exactly that.'

Joey sensed there was a lot behind that statement that Samuel Banning wasn't telling her. But, at the same time, there was a steely implacability about this man that left no room for doubt; he might be seventy-eight years old, but it was obvious that he still held firmly onto the reins of the family banking business. And that, no matter what impression David might try to give to the contrary, Samuel's word was law within that family...

'Thank you,' she accepted huskily.

Samuel smiled. 'You're more than welcome.'

Joey smiled back. She couldn't help herself, knew that, despite everything she might want to feel towards this family, she was starting to like Samuel and Lilian.

'Joey.' Lilian was the one to speak now. 'I want you to know we will never be able to express our gratitude to you for the way in which you have brought Lily up.' There were still tears in her eyes.

'I love her,' she replied simply.

'Yes.' Lilian swallowed hard. 'Can you ever—ever forgive Daniel for what he did six years ago? For walking out on you? For abandoning Lily? For—?' She broke off as Joey gave a pained gasp.

Joey turned to look at Nick as he stood up abruptly, his expression grim as he reached her side, sudden tears blinding her as his arms moved about her protectively.

'Obviously not,' Nick answered Lilian harshly. 'Perhaps it would be better if we continue this tomorrow?' His voice softened slightly. 'I think Joey has had enough for one evening.'

More than enough. But somehow she knew this wasn't over yet, that Lilian had more to say...

'I thought I knew my son.' Lilian spoke emotionally. 'I felt nothing but sympathy for him when he told me of the girl he had met at university. The girl he had loved. But I had no idea of Lily's existence, of the way he just shut her out of his life. I— Joey, can you ever forgive any of us for the way in which your sister died?'

Joey felt Nick's sudden tension as he still held her, could sense his complete puzzlement at Lilian Banning's last statement. With good reason!

Her sister...

Beautiful, fun-loving, carefree Josey.

Joanne and Josephine. Joey and Josey. Two sisters with only two years' difference in their ages. Probably because of their disruptive upbringing, their drunken father and downtrodden mother, they had had a closeness between them that had been unshakeable.

They had done everything together: shared a flat together once Joey was eighteen, found part-time jobs that allowed them both to attend university, Josey as a waitress, Joey as a hairdresser, had had the same friends, been free, at last, of their father's tyranny.

Then Josey had met Daniel Banning...

The love of her life, Josey had called him. And, while Joey hadn't quite shared her sister's wholehearted enthusiasm, she had liked Daniel.

Until Josey had announced that she was pregnant and Daniel had walked out on her.

There had followed months of heartache and tears—

Josey half convinced that Daniel would come back to her once their baby was born.

Daniel had come back, all right.

But only to attend Josey's funeral…

CHAPTER FIFTEEN

'WHY the hell didn't you tell me?' Nick demanded incredulously as Joey opened the front door to his ring.

She had known he would be back after driving the Bannings to a hotel for the night, had seen the shocked disbelief on his face as the truth had finally dawned on him. A truth that he had somehow managed not to let the Bannings see he hadn't already known...

That she wasn't actually Lily's mother. That it was her sister Josey. When the two sisters were at university, Josey taking a degree in English Literature while Joey did her Masters, it was Josey who had met and fallen in love with Daniel Banning.

'Come inside, Nick,' she invited softly, turning to go back into the sitting-room, handing him one of the two glasses of wine she had already poured as she waited for his return. She owed him an explanation, if nothing else.

But if Lilian and Samuel really meant all the things they had said to her a short time ago, before leaving—and Joey had no reason to think they didn't—then she owed Nick more than that. She now knew that her own method of dealing with this problem, of running away, would have been the wrong way.

'Cheers, Nick.' She held up her glass of wine in a toast before sipping at the ruby-red liquid. 'Why didn't I tell you?' She thoughtfully repeated his earlier question. 'What purpose would it have served? I might not have actually given birth to Lily, but in every other way that matters she is most assuredly my daughter.'

And Joey was willing to fight to the death to keep her. Although it looked as if she might not have to do that, after all...

She was still having trouble accepting that things really were going to work out, that Lilian and Samuel had suggested Joey legally adopt Lily, just so that her rights as Lily's 'mother' could never be taken away from her. Joey had known exactly what they meant by that; Lilian and Samuel wouldn't live for ever, and once they were gone David would take over as head of the Banning family...

'How did you find out about David?' She looked curiously at Nick as he still stood across the room from her.

'That he's unable to have children of his own?' Nick shrugged. 'My sister helped me with that one.'

Joey raised blonde brows as she frowned her puzzlement. 'Your sister?'

He nodded tersely. 'Joey, you still haven't told me why you didn't explain that Lily was actually your sister's child—'

'Because she isn't—she's mine!' she told him fiercely, fingers tight about the stem of her wine glass. 'There's more to being a mother than actually giving birth, you know!'

There was the constant care of a helpless baby, the sleepless nights and constant worry when she was ill, the nurturing, the feeding and clothing, the all-consuming loving...!

'I do know that, Joey,' he accepted gently, his expression softening. 'It just might have—helped if you had actually told me the truth from the beginning.'

'In what way?'

He made an impatient movement. 'In every way. Hell, Joey, I've been imagining all this time that you were in love with Daniel Banning! I even thought you were falling for David Banning because he looked like his younger brother!'

'Don't be ridiculous,' she dismissed incredulously.

'You talked to me of the pain of having lost someone you loved—'

'I was referring to Josey,' she interrupted quietly. 'We were more than just sisters; we were best friends as well. I even stayed on at university with her and started my Masters so that we could stay together. We were all each of us ever really had!' Her voice broke emotionally.

No one could ever imagine the pain she had known when her sister had lived only a matter of days after giving birth to Lily. Lily—a name chosen for her paternal grandmother, it now turned out! Joey had been bewildered by the loss, and then angry that her beautiful sister had been taken from her in this way. She hadn't even liked Daniel Banning then, had hated him with a vengeance, felt that Josey had just given up and died without him.

But Lily... It had only needed one look at the tiny, totally helpless creature that had been left in her care for Joey to love her with a fierce protectiveness.

That protectiveness had been what prompted her move from Oxford, where people knew both her and Josey from their years at university, and also knew that Lily was her sister Josey's child, not hers. She had wanted a fresh, uncomplicated start for both of them.

Although she had thought the past had caught up with her when David Banning arrived and called her Josey! It was luck, pure and simple luck, that the two sisters had had such similar names—that she'd been able to dismiss the mistake as exactly that. Even if it had resulted in David Banning casting aspersions upon her writing capabilities! A small price to pay, in the circumstances.

'As for "all this time",' Joey repeated impatiently, 'we've only known each other just over a week, Nick!'

He shook his head. 'It seems like much longer than that,' he acknowledged ruefully.

Joey smiled slightly. 'Doesn't it just?'

Nick grinned. 'You had me worried earlier when you told me you were never going to forgive me for bringing the Bannings here.'

'I'm deferring judgement on that until after my adoption of Lily is made final,' she told him drily.

He sobered. 'It's the right thing to do, you know. And with the senior Bannings' wholehearted agreement to the arrangement, there are sure to be no legal problems.'

Joey shook her head. 'I still can't believe David only suggested marrying me because he knows he's incapable of ever providing an heir of his own. As Lily's stepfather he would have been in total control of the Banning fortune once Lilian and Samuel...' she broke off emotionally. 'He knew his parents well enough to realise that once they were made aware of Lily's existence they would confer Daniel's inheritance on to her!'

'Now that he's been made aware of the situation, I have no doubts that Samuel is more than capable of controlling David,' Nick assured her grimly. 'They really are horrified at the machinations he attempted to try and take control of the only other Banning heir besides himself.' He shook his head disgustedly. 'How could such nice people have had two such totally selfish sons?'

Joey had wondered that herself. But perhaps that was the explanation: Samuel and Lilian were two genuinely nice people who had over-indulged their two sons to the point where they'd become emotional tyrants.

'It doesn't matter any more,' she dismissed with renewed relief. 'All that's ever mattered to me is that Lily stays with me.' And loving this man to the point where she felt an ache in her chest just looking at him!

But that was another issue completely.

One that she knew wasn't going to have such a happy ending...

'I really am grateful to you, Nick,' she told him warmly. 'None of this would be happening without your help.'

'Hey, I think Lily is pretty wonderful too,' he assured her indulgently.

She nodded. 'But you went out of your way...' She stopped, shaking her head, the tears threatening to fall. 'I still can't believe it's all over!' Her voice broke emotionally.

From feelings of complete helplessness she now felt complete euphoria. Lily would never be taken from her now!

She owed it to Josey to one day tell her daughter the truth, but that was a long way in the future—would happen at a time when she knew Lily was old enough to understand, and accept.

'I'm sorry,' she told Nick as the tears began to fall hotly down her cheeks. 'It's just—I'm so happy!'

Nick moved forward to gather her into his arms. 'I'd hate to see what reaction you have when you're miserable!' He spoke teasingly into the silky thickness of her hair.

Joey gave a hiccuping laugh against the warmth of his chest. As she knew she was supposed to.

How she loved this man! Loved his tenderness, his caring, his strength. She just loved everything about him.

'I actually don't get miserable—I come out fighting,' she told him ruefully.

'Don't I know it?' Nick shook his head indulgently. 'You've given me more than my fair share of bad moments,' he explained at her questioning look. 'But I want you to know, Joey, that I would never have let the Banning family take Lily away from you. Not without one hell of a fight,' he added grimly. 'I actually went to New York with the intention of evaluating the enemy. But my initial meeting with Lilian and Samuel told me that they didn't have a clue what David was up to.'

Joey shuddered as she recalled the desolation David's threats had caused in her this last week. 'I really thought for a while that I was going to lose Lily, you know.' She still quaked at the thought of how close she had come to falling straight into the trap David Banning had set for her with his proposal of marriage.

'It will never happen,' Nick assured her harshly. 'But tell me, Joey,' his voice softened huskily, 'wouldn't you ever like a child of your own?'

She stiffened. 'Lily—'

'Is your child,' Nick finished. 'I know that, Joey. And she always will be a very special child. But wouldn't you like to know the joy of carrying your own child, of giving birth, of—?'

'Unfortunately, you have to find a man to love, who loves you in return, to be able to do that,' Joey told him drily, moving away from him as she pulled out of his arms. 'And I don't have that. Which reminds me...' She looked down at the emerald and diamond ring she wore on her left hand. 'You may as well have this back now.'

'Keep it,' Nick rasped as she would have removed the ring from her finger.

Joey hesitated, looking up at him uncertainly, but she could read nothing from his closed expression. 'I couldn't, Nick.' She shook her head ruefully. 'It was only ever on loan—'

'I said keep it!' he bit out fiercely as she would have removed the ring completely. 'Joey.' He forced calmness into his voice as she stared at him with wide green eyes. 'I...' He sighed. 'Couldn't we...? Now that the problem of Lily is resolved, couldn't we start again?'

She frowned her puzzlement. 'In what way?'

He shrugged. 'I ask you out to dinner. You accept. We have a nice evening together. I invite you out again. You accept. And so on and so on?'

She moistened dry lips, her breathing once again feeling constricted. 'You want to invite me out?' She finally managed to speak.

'I want much more than that!' he assured her impatiently. 'But I can wait. I think,' he added wryly.

'Nick, I—I think perhaps you have the wrong idea about me.' She grimaced. 'I may be a single mother, and my options may be limited, but I have no intention—I wouldn't share you!' she told him bluntly.

'"Share me"?' he repeated frowningly. 'Share me with whom?'

Joey swallowed hard. 'I... Well—Barbara Dillon, for one!' she finally managed to burst out.

'With Barbara...?' Nick repeated, dumbfounded.

Well, at least he wasn't trying to deny his relationship with the other woman! But even so... 'David had you followed,' she revealed awkwardly. 'He took great delight in telling me that you were having dinner on Saturday evening with a beautiful woman named Barbara Dillon.'

'Did he, indeed?' Nick mused hardly.

Really, this was just too embarrassing. Nick was only inviting her to have dinner with him, not proposing! But, even so, she was in love with the man. She did not want to become part of some damned harem!

And the fact that Nick now appeared to be laughing did not improve her temper one little bit!

'This isn't funny, Nick,' she snapped uncomfortably.

'I agree, it isn't.' He sobered slightly. 'But I'm sure my sister will very much enjoy being referred to as a ''beautiful woman''!'

Now it was Joey's turn to stare at him dumbfounded. His sister? 'But her name is Dillon—'

'It's Barbara's married name,' he explained lightly. 'I'm sure I told you she was divorced when I mentioned that her opinion of men more or less matched your own? Her ex-husband instilled that into her.' He grimaced. 'But she is my sister, Joey. I told you she works on a newspaper. I spoke to her about Banning because she knows a lot of people—and a lot about people. And what she doesn't know, she can usually find out,' he said.

'Like the fact that David Banning can't have children of his own,' Joey realised dazedly.

'Exactly,' Nick said with satisfaction. 'Which led me to realising exactly why he wanted to be Lily's stepfather,' he added hardly. 'Look, I'll introduce Barbara to you, if you like,' he suggested as Joey continued to look uncomfortable.

'That won't be necessary,' she returned stiffly. Talk about feeling a fool...!

But how could she possibly have known that Barbara Dillon was the divorced older sister Nick had talked about? She couldn't, she instantly assured herself. But she could have given Nick the benefit of the doubt...

'Oh, I think it will be very necessary,' Nick told her softly. 'I want you, and Lily, to meet all of my family— including the monstrous Dominic Mason Senior!' he added teasingly.

Joey looked at him uncertainly. 'Why?'

He shrugged. 'Because you're all nice people.'

'Oh.' She could hardly contain her disappointment.

But what had she expected—a declaration of undying

love? She might have fallen in love with Nick, but that didn't mean he would ever return the feeling.

'How's the packing going, Joey?'

She was totally stunned by the sudden change of subject, blinking across at him dazedly. 'It was going well,' she admitted distractedly. 'But I suppose I may as well start unpacking again now,' she realised, once again feeling exhilarated by the fact that there was no need to run now. No reason for her ever to need to run again.

Lily was hers. Was going to remain hers. It was going to take some time for that to fully sink in.

'Why don't you leave it for a while?' Nick suggested gruffly.

'Why?' She frowned.

'Joey, I know this has been a very special day for you,' he said frustratedly, 'but have you been listening to anything I've had to say?'

Of course she had been listening. He wanted to invite her out. Was hoping she would accept. That they would enjoy each other's company. And if they did then he would ask her out again. She didn't see how that affected her unpacking.

'Joey.' He moved a step towards her, lightly grasping the tops of her arms. 'You are a very special woman. An exceptionally special woman,' he corrected. 'I can't think of too many women who would have done what you did—give up any idea of your own life and university career in order to take care of your niece.' He shook his head admiringly.

'But—'

'But it isn't just that that makes you exceptional,' Nick continued firmly as she would have interrupted. 'You're kind, caring, considerate—'

'I—'

'And it isn't only those things that make me love you,' he continued determinedly over her second interruption. 'You're beautiful, inside as well as out. Totally unselfish. Totally without guile.' He shook his head in amazement. 'I've never met anyone like you before, Joey.'

Her breath was lodged in her throat as she stared up at him, completely unable to speak now. Nick loved her?

He winced self-consciously as she could only stare up at him. 'It's too soon,' he admonished himself impatiently. 'I hadn't meant to say that just yet.' He shook his head self-disgustedly. 'You're right. We've only known each other just over a week—'

'I think I knew how I felt about you within a few minutes of meeting you.' Joey finally spoke huskily, happiness such as she had never known before welling up inside her.

This couldn't be happening to her. She couldn't finally be secure about Lily and have the man she loved on the same day!

Nick's throat moved convulsively. 'And how do you feel about me?' he prompted gruffly.

She gave a shaky smile. 'I'm in love with you.'

Nick fell back a step, breathing heavily, obviously totally stunned.

Joey gave a rueful half-smile. 'Add totally honest to that earlier list of character traits!'

Too honest for her own good? Nick certainly seemed to have been shocked into silence by her words!

'Nick…?' she voiced uncertainly when she could stand his silence no longer.

He drew in a long, rasping breath, as if he were the one who had now forgotten to breathe for a while. 'Will you marry me, Joanne Delaney? Will you continue to wear my engagement ring until I can place a gold wedding band at its side?'

Joey's heart soared with happiness. 'As long as you'll let me put a gold wedding band on your hand too.' She nodded shyly.

'Oh, yes!' he assured her with certainty as he put his arms about her, gently kissing her forehead, each of her eyes, the tip of her nose, before his mouth finally claimed hers.

Home. She was finally home. Nick's arms were her home...

'He's very beautiful, Mummy.' Lily looked down in awe at her hours-old baby brother.

'Very beautiful,' Joey agreed happily, tired after the birth, but also filled with a euphoria that was beyond description.

'Not as beautiful as Mummy.' Nick spoke gruffly at her side, his hand tightening on hers as they watched Lily's gentle caress of her brother's creamy brow as he lay fast asleep in his crib. 'I love you, Joanne Mason,' he told her with feeling.

She smiled up at him. 'And I love you.' She reached up to kiss him lingeringly on the lips, pleased to have had him at her side all the way through her pregnancy and their son's birth, to see the love and pride almost bursting out of him as he held Adam for the first time. Since meeting Nick her life had just seemed to get better and better. 'I love all of you so much.' Her glowing gaze encompassed all of her family.

And they were a family, had been so for a year now— a year of complete happiness, a year when both she and Nick had quietly, with Lilian and Samuel's blessing, adopted Lily for their own.

As promised, Lilian and Samuel had dealt with the problem of David, had tied up the future of the Banning fortune so tightly David would never be a threat to Lily again. In fact, Lilian and Samuel had been absolutely wonderful this last year, and Joey, Nick and Lily had spent New Year with them. As honorary grandparents to Adam, the other couple would be flying over from New York tomorrow to see the new arrival.

Joey was constantly amazed at how well everything had turned out. It had been no hardship for her to give her business to Hilary when she moved to London after marrying Nick, and, despite several reservations about moving Lily, their young daughter had blossomed in the centre of her new family.

Nick's parents both loved Lily, but amazingly it was Nick's sister Barbara who had fallen completely under Lily's spell. So much so that she was even considering marrying the man she had been involved with the last three years, aching to have a child of their own. Joey didn't doubt Adam's arrival would make that ache all the stronger!

Nick bent down to kiss her. 'I can't wait to have you and Adam home again.' His love shone in his deep brown eyes.

'Oh, yes,' she breathed happily.

Home.

Because home was wherever she and Nick were.

Together.

Joey had no doubts that she really had found her own Mr Right…

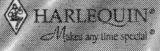

If you enjoyed what you just read,
then we've got an offer you can't resist!

Take 2 bestselling love stories FREE!

Plus get a FREE surprise gift!

Clip this page and mail it to Harlequin Reader Service®

IN U.S.A.	IN CANADA
3010 Walden Ave.	P.O. Box 609
P.O. Box 1867	Fort Erie, Ontario
Buffalo, N.Y. 14240-1867	L2A 5X3

YES! Please send me 2 free Harlequin Romance® novels and my free surprise gift. After receiving them, if I don't wish to receive anymore, I can return the shipping statement marked cancel. If I don't cancel, I will receive 6 brand-new novels every month, before they're available in stores! In the U.S.A., bill me at the bargain price of $3.34 plus 25¢ shipping & handling per book and applicable sales tax, if any*. In Canada, bill me at the bargain price of $3.80 plus 25¢ shipping & handling per book and applicable taxes**. That's the complete price and a savings of 10% off the cover prices—what a great deal! I understand that accepting the 2 free books and gift places me under no obligation ever to buy any books. I can always return a shipment and cancel at any time. Even if I never buy another book from Harlequin, the 2 free books and gift are mine to keep forever.

186 HDN DNTX
386 HDN DNTY

Name	(PLEASE PRINT)	
Address	Apt.#	
City	State/Prov.	Zip/Postal Code

* Terms and prices subject to change without notice. Sales tax applicable in N.Y.
** Canadian residents will be charged applicable provincial taxes and GST.
 All orders subject to approval. Offer limited to one per household and not valid to current Harlequin Romance® subscribers.
® are registered trademarks of Harlequin Enterprises Limited.

HROM02   ©2001 Harlequin Enterprises Limited

$ Saving Money $ Has Never Been This Easy!

Just fill out and send in this form from any October, November and December 2002 books and we will send you a coupon booklet worth a total savings of $20.00 off future purchases of Harlequin and Silhouette books in 2003.

Yes! It's that easy!

**I accept your incredible offer!
Please send me a coupon booklet:**

Name (PLEASE PRINT)

Address _____ Apt. #

City _____ State/Prov. _____ Zip/Postal Code

**In a typical month, how many
Harlequin and Silhouette novels do you read?**

❏ 0-2   ❏ 3+

097KJKDNC7   097KJKDNDP

Please send this form to:
   In the U.S.: Harlequin Books, P.O. Box 9071, Buffalo, NY 14269-9071
   In Canada: Harlequin Books, P.O. Box 609, Fort Erie, Ontario L2A 5X3

Allow 4-6 weeks for delivery. Limit one coupon booklet per household. Must be postmarked no later than January 15, 2003.

HARLEQUIN®
Makes any time special®

Silhouette®
Where love comes alive™